Ghostly Paws

Leighann Dobbs

Copyright

This is a work of fiction.
None of it is real. All names, places, and events are products of the author's imagination. Any resemblance to real names, places, or events are purely coincidental, and should not be construed as being real.

Cover art by: http://www.coverkicks.com

Chapter One

In over thirty years as head librarian for the Mystic Notch Library, Lavinia Babbage had never once opened the doors before eight a.m.

I knew this because my bookstore sat across the street and three doors down from the library. Every day, I passed its darkened windows on my way to work. I watched Lavinia turn on the lights and open the doors every single morning at precisely eight a.m. from inside my shop.

Most days I didn't pay much attention to the library, though. It was really the last thing on my mind as I walked past, my mind set on sorting through a large box of books I'd purchased at an estate sale earlier in the week. The edges of my lips curled in a smile as I thought about the gold placard I'd had installed on the oak door of the old bookshop just the day before. *Wilhelmina Chance, Proprietor.* That made things official—the shop was mine and I was back in my hometown, Mystic Notch, to stay.

I hurried down the street, deep in my own thoughts. The early morning mist, which wrapped itself around our sleepy town in the White Mountains of New Hampshire, had caused the pain to flare in my leg, and I forced myself not to limp. I continued along, my head down and engrossed in my thoughts when I nearly tripped over something gray and furry. My cat, Pandora, had stopped short in front of me causing me to do a painful sidestep to avoid squashing her.

"Hey, what the heck?"

Pandora blinked her golden-green eyes at me and jerked her head toward the library ... or at least it seemed like she did. Cats didn't actually jerk their heads toward things, though, did they?

Of course they didn't.

I looked in the direction of the library anyway. That's when I noticed the beam of light spilling onto the granite steps from the half-open library door.

Which was odd, since it was only ten past seven.

My stomach started to feel queasy. Lavinia never opened up this early. Should I venture in to check it out? Maybe Lavinia had come in early to catch up on restocking the bookshelves before the library opened. But she never left the door open like that, she was as strict as a nun about keeping that door closed.

I stood on the sidewalk, staring at the medieval-looking stone library building, my pre-caffeine fog making it difficult for me to decide what to do.

Pandora had no such trouble deciding. She raced up the steps past me. With a flick of her gray tail, she darted toward the massive oak door, shooting a reproachful look at me over her shoulder before disappearing into the building.

I took a deep breath and followed her inside.

"Lavinia? You in here?" My words echoed inside the library as I pushed the heavy oak door open, its hinges groaning eerily. The library was as still as a morgue with only the sound of the grandfather clock marking time in the corner broke the silence.

"Lavinia? You okay?"

No one answered.

I crept past the old oak desk, stacked with books ready to return to the library shelves. The bronze bust of Franklin Pierce, fourteenth president of the United States, glared at me from the end of the hall. I didn't have a good feeling about this.

"Meow." The sound came from the back corner where the stone steps lead to the lower level. Dammit! I'd warned Lavinia about those steps. They were steep and she wasn't that steady on her feet anymore.

I headed toward the back, my heart sinking as I noticed Lavinia's cane lying at the top of the stairs.

"Lavinia?" Rounding the corner, my stomach dropped when I saw a crumpled heap at the bottom of the stairs ... Lavinia.

I raced down the steps two at a time, my heart pounding as I took in the scene. Blood on the steps. Lavinia laying there, blood in her gray hair. She'd fallen and taken it hard on the way down. But she could still be alive.

I bent down beside her, taking her wrist between my fingers and checking for a pulse.

Lavinia's head tilted at a strange angle. Her glassy eyes stared toward the room where she kept new book arrivals before cataloguing them. I dropped her wrist, ending my search for a pulse.

Lavinia Babbage had stamped her last library book.

***

I called my sister Augusta, or Gus as I called her, who also happened to be the sheriff, and sat on the steps to wait. I might have drifted off, still sleepy from the lack of caffeine, because the next thing I heard was Augusta's voice in my ear.

"Willa, are you okay?"

I opened one eye to the welcome sight of the steaming Styrofoam coffee cup that Gus was holding out to me.

"I'm fine," I said, reaching for the cup.

"What happened?" I studied Gus who stood on the steps in front of me. No one would have guessed we were sisters. She was petite, her long, straight blonde hair tied back in a ponytail, which, I assume, she thought made her look more sheriff-like. Even in the un-flattering sheriff's uniform, you could tell she had an almost perfect hourglass figure. I was tall with thick wavy red hair, my figure more rounded—voluptuous, as some described me. The only thing we had in common was our amber colored eyes—same as our mom's.

"I was on my way to open the bookstore when I noticed the lights on in the library." I glanced down the street toward the municipal parking lot.

Now that the spring warm-up was here, I was trying to work in some extra exercise by parking in the lot two blocks away instead of on the street near the bookstore.

"Was that unusual?" Gus asked.

"Yep." I looked over my shoulder at the front door of the library. "It sure was. Lavinia never opens the library before eight. Plus the front door was cracked open, and she never leaves it open."

Gus started up the steps toward the library. "Did you touch anything?"

I stood up, wincing at the pain in my left leg—a reminder of the near fatal accident over a year ago that was one of the catalysts for my move back to Mystic Notch. The accident had left me with a slight limp, a bunch of scars and a few odd side effects I didn't like to dwell on.

"Nope, other than Lavinia. I didn't know if she was alive and needed aid," I said as I followed Gus into the library.

Gus stopped just inside the door and looked around. The coppery smell of blood tinged the air, making me lose interest in my coffee.

"It doesn't seem like anything is out of place ... no sign of struggle," she said.

"Nope, I think she just fell down the stairs." I started toward the back. "You know she was getting on in years and not that steady on her feet."

We turned the corner and my stomach clenched at the sight of Lavinia at the bottom of the steps.

"That's her cane?" Gus pointed to the purple metal cane, which was still lying as I'd found it.

"Yep. Looks like she lost her balance, dropped the cane, and fell."

Gus descended the stairs, her eyes carefully taking in every detail. She knelt beside Lavinia, studying her head. "She's pretty banged up."

"I know. These stairs are hard stone. I guess they can do a number on you." I winced as I looked at the bloody edges of the steps.

"So, you think this was an accident?"

"Sure. I mean, what else could have happened?"

"Yeah, you're probably right. No reason to suspect foul play." Gus stood and looked back up the stairs, down the hall and then back at Lavinia.

Her lips were pressed in a thin line and I wondered what she was thinking. I knew she was a good cop, but the truth was I didn't really know her all that well. Eight years separated us and she was just a teenager when I'd moved down south. Now, twenty-five years later, we were just becoming acquainted as adults.

"Mew." Pandora sat on the empty table in the storage room where Lavinia temporarily stored new books or returns before she catalogued them. I'd forgotten she was here. She wasn't really my cat ... well, not until recently. I'd inherited her along with the bookstore and my grandmother's house. I still wasn't used to being followed around by a feline.

"Isn't that Pandora?" Gus asked. Gus had been close to grandma—closer than I had, and it was somewhat of a mystery that Grandma had left me the shop, her house and the cat. In her will, she'd said she'd wanted me to come back home and have a house and business, which was odd because the timing had been perfect. She'd left a tidy sum of money for Gus, so at least there were no hard feelings.

"Yeah, she rides to work with me."

Gus raised a brow at me, but didn't say anything. Pandora stared at us—her intelligent, greenish-gold eyes contrasting eerily with her sleek gray fur.

"So, if it was unusual for Lavinia to be here at this time of the morning, why do you think she was here and what do you think she was doing?" Gus asked.

"I'm not sure."

Gus reached out to pet Pandora, who still sat on the table staring at us. "Are there any mice in here, Pandora? Maybe Lavinia heard something down here and wanted to investigate."

"Maybe." I looked around the floor for evidence of mice. Lavinia ran a pretty tight ship so I doubted there would be any mice in the library. And, since the room was empty of books, she hadn't come in early to catalogue new arrivals.

Which begged the question ... why *was* Lavinia in the library this early in the first place?

Chapter Two

The EMT's and Gus's deputy arrived and got busy with their crime scene investigation. After Gus asked me the standard questions and had the nerve to tell me not to leave town, I headed down the street to open the bookstore.

The crowd of four 'regulars' were already waiting outside, their necks craning to see what was going on at the library.

You wouldn't think a bookstore would have regulars, but mine did. Apparently, I'd inherited them, along with the store and the cat. They'd been gathering there in the mornings with their coffee and tea for decades. I guess the coffee shop down the street didn't have the same ambiance.

"What's going on down there?" Cordelia Deering looked at me with bright sparkling blue eyes. Her twin sister Hattie, stood beside her and, dressed almost identically, gave me the exact same look of expectant excitement. The women were in their mid-eighties, but had more energy than people who were decades younger. They were always up for hearing a tidbit of juicy gossip and liked to keep up on town happenings. This particular happening, though, I hoped wouldn't be too much of a shock.

"I'm afraid I have some bad news," I said as I dug the key out of my pocket and put it in the shiny brass lock of the antique oak door of the bookshop.

"Oh?" Bingham Thorndike, another of the regulars, raised a bushy white brow.

I pushed the door open and gestured for them to go inside. Cordelia and Hattie went first, then Josiah Barrows, the retired Postmaster, then Bingham, or Bing as we all called him.

They all looked at me expectantly as I turned the sign in the door to 'Open' and switched on the inside lights. I took a deep breath of the comforting musky-vanilla scent of leather and old paper.

"So, what's going on down at the library?" Josiah broke the silence. I was surprised he didn't already know since he seemed to know everything that went on in town, sometimes even before it actually happened.

"I'm afraid Lavinia took a fall." I bit my lower lip and tried to figure out a gentle way to break the news. After a few seconds, I hadn't come up with anything so I just blurted it out. "She's dead."

Hattie and Cordelia gasped. Bing sipped his coffee. Josiah rubbed his chin. Pandora jumped up on the counter next to my nickel-plated old-fashioned cash register and let out a mournful wail.

"Mercy sakes," Hattie said as she maneuvered her way past the chair toward the sofa.

"Poor Lavinia," Cordelia whispered.

I'd recently added a set of purple micro-suede chairs and a sofa to the front of the shop for customers who wanted to sit and read a book while browsing. The four of them settled somberly into the plush seating.

I watched them sip from their Styrofoam cups, their faces in thoughtful repose. They looked comfortable on the sofa. At home. I started to wonder if maybe I had made it *too* comfortable for them.

"You sure she fell?" Josiah wrinkled his brow at me.

I nodded. "She was getting up in years and not so steady anymore. I found her at the bottom of the stairs—the ones in the back."

"You found her? What were you doing in the library?" Bing asked.

I explained how I'd seen the light on, gone in to investigate and found her lying at the bottom of the steps. I left out the part about all the blood.

"Oh dear, that must have been terrible for you," Cordelia clucked.

"That must have happened early on." Josiah scrunched up his weathered old face. "In all my years as postmaster, I don't recall Lavinia ever gettin' to the library before eight o'clock."

"That's true," Hattie and Cordelia said at the same time, then looked at each other and giggled.

"Seems odd she fell. She got along pretty good every time I saw her around town," Josiah added.

"But it must have been a fall," Bing said. "No one would want Lavinia dead."

I half-listened as the four of them rambled on about the subject, distracted by the swirling gray mist that was forming over by the mystery section. A prickly feeing of uneasiness settled over me—I knew what that gray mist was.

Pandora hopped off the counter and trotted over to the mist, batting at it playfully.

"Right, Willa?" Bing's question tore my attention away from the swirly mist.

"Huh?"

"Lavinia came in early sometimes when she had a backlog of returns or books to catalogue."

I thought about the question as I watched Bing weave a large gold coin in between his fingers. A retired magician, he was always fiddling with coins and doing impromptu tricks with various objects. I'd known Bing since I was a little girl, and he taught me a few of his tricks. Some of them I still practiced, but there were quite a few more of them, the ones he wouldn't teach me, that had me baffled. I couldn't figure out how he did them. It was almost as if he really was using magic.

The effect of the coin was mesmerizing. I watched it weave in front of his index finger, then behind his middle finger, then in front of the Magicians Guild ring he wore on his ring finger then behind the pinkie and around, making its way all the way back to his index finger. As I watched, I contemplated his question. Had Lavinia come in early sometimes? I was having a hard time remembering.

"I'm not sure, Bing. I can't remember." I looked at Josiah. "Do you remember, Josiah?"

Josiah looked like he was about to nod off. He tilted his head and looked up at the ceiling. I was about to prompt him again when he finally spoke.

"I can't say for sure. I think one time she did come in early but that was before a big book sale," he said. "Was she fixing to have a book sale?"

We all looked at each other and shrugged.

"I have no idea," Hattie said.

"We could look in the Gazette," Cordelia said, referring to the town paper. "There would be an announcement if she was planning one this week."

Out of the corner of my eye, the mist was getting thicker. It swirled around the edge of the bookcase, beckoning to me. Pandora sat next to it, her eyes drilling into mine.

Bing drained his coffee and pushed up off the couch. "Well, I gotta be on my way. Lots to do today."

"Me, too," Josiah said.

"I guess the party's over." Cordelia stood. "We'll let you get to work, Willa. Let us know if you find out anything more about Lavinia."

"Will do," I said as I watched them file out the door.

As soon as they were gone, I turned my attention to the misty swirl. The swirl was one of the side effects of my accident—the one I didn't like to dwell on. But, I'd found out the hard way that if I ignored it, things only got worse.

So, I straightened my shoulders and walked toward it.

I marched past the rows of books to the end of the aisle. Rounding the corner, my breath caught in my throat as I came face to face with ... Lavinia Babbage.

***

"Eeek!" Lavinia screeched, her ghost turning to static like an off-air channel on an old television set.

"Lavinia!" I squawked, my heart thumping in my chest. I knew the swirl meant a ghost was around the corner, but I wasn't expecting it to be *Lavinia's* ghost.

Ever since my accident, I'd been seeing ghosts. It started off as just random sightings of misty swirls. Then the swirls started to form into human shapes. Then they started talking to me. It wasn't something I wanted, it just happened ... and it was impossible to ignore them. Each one of them seemed to want something and would pester me until they got it. I wondered what Lavinia wanted.

"Sorry, Willa," she said, her form materializing into a semi-solid shape. "I wasn't expecting you to come barreling around the corner like that. And I'm sorry you had to find me ... you know ... at the library."

"Oh. Right. Sorry you ... umm ... died."

"Thanks." She held her hand up toward the window and we both watched the sunlight filter through it. Lavinia waffled her hand back and forth, apparently fascinated with the effect.

"So, did you want something?" I prompted as I glanced over my shoulder into the shop, praying no customers would come in and find me talking to thin air.

She put her hand down. "Yes, sorry, I'm still getting used to being dead. It's not easy, you know."

"I'm sure it's not."

"Anyway, I didn't fall down the steps."

I was afraid she was going to say something like that. "What do you mean?"

"I mean I didn't trip and fall. I got whacked on the back of the head and was pushed!"

"Pushed? Are you sure?"

"Sure as shinola," Lavinia said, then leaned forward and lowered her voice. "I was on my way to church to … umm … light a candle for my Harry. I often did that before opening the library. Anyway, I was on my way when I saw the lights on in the library. I knew I didn't leave them on, so I went in to investigate. I thought I heard something downstairs, but as I approached the steps, I heard something behind me. I turned to see what it was and then … whack! Lights out!"

"You didn't see who it was? Did you get any sense of whether it was a man or woman?"

"Nope. All I saw was a big shadow … like the person was wearing a cape." Lavinia pressed her lips together and looked out the window. "Oh, and they wore a big ring."

"Ring? What kind of ring?"

She looked back at me, her ghostly form rippling like water disturbed by a pebble. "I'm not sure. It was chunky, like a class ring. I remember hearing the noise, seeing the shadow, feeling pain and getting pushed. I saw the ring in a blur as I went down. Next thing I know, I'm waking up on a steel table inside Stilton's funeral home. Scared me half to death. Of course, I didn't realize I actually *was* dead at first. Anyway, once I figured it all out, I knew I had to come here and get your help."

"You did? How did you know to come to me?" I felt a little disturbed by this. Was there some sort of sign in the afterlife telling these ghosts to seek me out? I certainly hoped not.

Lavinia tilted her head. "You know, I'm not rightly sure about that. Might be because I know you were a crime journalist down south. Anyway, I just got this feeling and it must have been right because you're the only person that's been able to see and talk to me since I ... err... died."

"Okay. Well, I'm not sure what you think I can do for you. I didn't see any evidence of anyone being there in the library. Maybe you're confused about what happened, you know—with being so newly dead and all?" I asked hopefully.

"No, I don't think so. I'm sure someone did me in."

"But, *who* would break into the library and why would they want to kill you?"

"I have no idea," Lavinia said. "That's for *you* to find out. All I know is that I need your help to find the killer and neither one of us is going to be able to rest until you do.

Chapter Three

Lavinia's ghost started to fade, her final words barely above a whisper. "Only *you* can help me, Willa."

Pandora batted at the last trailing wisp of ghost mist, then looked up at me and meowed something that sounded like, "*You have to help.*"

I frowned down at the cat. "Did you just say—?"

My words were cut off by the sound of the bells over the door. I looked between the bookcases in time to see Pepper St. Onge bustle in carrying a silver tray complete with teapot and two porcelain teacups on dainty saucers. She wore a cute vintage skirt set in violet, which complemented the mass of auburn hair piled on top of her head. Pepper usually wore her hair up like that. She'd been growing it since kindergarten, where we'd met and become best friends. Last I knew it fell below her waist. My heart warmed thinking of our close friendship that had lasted for forty-three years, even though I'd spent almost half of those years "down south" in Massachusetts.

"I heard what happened at the library, so I figured you could use a nice calming cup of tea." Pepper peered down the aisle at me as she put the tray down on the coffee table.

She settled her tall, slim frame onto the couch, then patted the seat beside her as an invitation for me to sit.

"Thanks."

I sat beside her and she poured the tea, then added a splash of cream from the tiny silver creamer she'd brought.

"I put something a little special in there to calm your nerves," she said as she handed me a pink chintz cup perched atop its matching saucer.

I looked into the cup dubiously. Pepper had fallen in love with herbal teas when we were in high school. It was no surprise to me when she opened a tea room in our small hometown. People came from all over New England to drink tea and eat finger sandwiches and cakes in her cozy shop. Pepper claimed that her teas had healing powers.

At first, I had thought she was just being fanciful, but after witnessing several examples of her healing teas in action, I believed they *did* have some sort of powers. The problem was that they usually backfired and had the opposite effect than was intended.

I sipped the tea politely, wondering if it would have the opposite effect and make me more anxious.

Pepper watched me from over the rim of her teacup. My heart warmed at the concern in her emerald green eyes.

"How did you find out about Lavinia already?" I asked.

"The twins stopped by for a bag of peppermint tea," she said, referring to Hattie and Cordelia.

"Ahh..." I nodded sagely. The grapevine in our small town worked quickly, so I wasn't surprised that word had gotten out already.

"So, what happened?"

She clucked with sympathy as I told her how I'd seen the library door open and light on and then found Lavinia at the bottom of the stairs.

"And that's not even the worst part," I said.

"Oh?" Her brows crept up her forehead.

"Lavinia's ghost claims she was pushed."

"Ohhh." Pepper's eyes grew wide. She was the only one I'd told about my strange new ability and was fascinated with it. "What did she tell you?"

"Just that someone hit her on the head and then pushed her, and she won't rest until I find whoever did it," I said.

"And you're going to find whoever did it?"

"I don't have much of a choice, because I know that when she says she won't rest, it really means that *I* won't rest because she'll keep pestering me."

"So what's your plan? Did she give you any clues?"

"Two clues. The person was wearing a cape and had a big ring."

Pepper frowned. "A cape? Like a super hero?"

I laughed. "More like a super villain. I'm not sure if her account is reliable ... she only saw a shadow of the killer and their hand, so I think it could have been just a loose coat they were wearing. I mean, who wears a cape?"

Pepper sipped her tea. "So what are you going to do?"

I sighed, leaning back on the couch. I was starting to feel more relaxed—maybe Pepper's tea had worked its healing magic as intended this time.

"Well, I guess first I'll have to ask the other shop owners if they saw anyone around the library early this morning," I said. "Not too many people are here at that time."

"I know Myrna comes in to the coffee shop early," Pepper said. "Maybe she saw something?"

I glanced out the window toward the coffee shop. "I'll pop down and ask her later. Lavinia said she was lighting a candle at church and that's why she was here early. Maybe Pastor Foley saw someone."

"What about the police?" Pepper started to stack the teacups back on the tray. "Surely they'll investigate?"

"Yeah, that's the problem," I said. "It *looks* like Lavinia fell. I thought that's what happened and I'm sure Augusta thought so, too. So, unless something comes to light, I don't think there'll be an investigation."

"But, Lavinia told you—"

"Not Lavinia," I said, cutting her off. "Lavinia's *ghost*. And who's going to believe I found out about the murder from her ghost? Nobody. In fact, it's probably better if I don't say anything to the police. I have a funny feeling that if I did, it would only point the finger of suspicion at *me*."

***

I woke up to Pandora digging her razor sharp claws into me. In my dream, I swore she was talking. *Get up now. Now. Now.*

"Meow. Meow. Meow."

"Ouch!" Pandora was crouched on my chest. I swatted her away before her claw ripped a hole in my black knit turtleneck.

I glanced at my watch. Noon! Had I really fallen asleep in my bookstore?

I sat up and wiped the drool off my cheek. Good thing no customers had come in. Or maybe they had come and found me sleeping.

Pandora trotted over to the large front window, hopped up onto the wide ledge where one of her overstuffed cat beds sat and stared pointedly down the street.

My eyes followed her gaze straight to the coffee shop—*The Mystic Cafe*. Come to think of it, I *was* getting a little hungry. The cafe had a great selection of sandwiches. I could close up for lunch, get something to eat and drink ... and ask Myrna if she saw anyone this morning.

I pushed up from the couch and wiped the cat hair off my sweater, then grabbed my wallet, locked the bookstore and headed down the street. I was halfway to the cafe before I realized my leg wasn't even hurting anymore. I felt thankful that the pain was slowly lessening with time.

The Mystic Cafe was abuzz with activity. Almost all the local merchants came here for lunch. It was off-season now—too late for the crowds that came for skiing and too early for summer tourists, so the cafe wasn't quite as crowded.

I made my way to the counter, nodding at the locals I knew, which was most everyone in there, seeing as I'd grown up here and most people didn't leave Mystic Notch. Ever.

I was the exception, going "down south" as they called it, to become a journalist. I felt a pinch in my chest at the thought of my former life. Best not to think about that now. Fate had stepped in and I was happy to be home again and starting a new life at the age of forty-eight.

As I walked through the cafe, I caught myself sneaking a peek at people's hands to see if anyone was wearing a large ring. What was I doing? These were my friends and neighbors. A shiver went up my spine as I realized that anyone could be the killer—even someone I trusted and had known my whole life.

Myrna Littleton stood behind the counter, her gray hair piled in a bun, her vintage red cherries apron barely covering her plump figure.

"What can I get'cha, Willa?" Myrna pulled a pencil out of her bun and poised it over the long pad of paper she held.

"I'll have a tuna on rye ... and if you have a second, I've got a few questions."

Myrna wrote down the order, ripped the paper off the pad and clipped it onto a round metal holder, then twirled it so the order was facing Bud, the guy who made the sandwiches in the back.

Her steely gaze assessed the crowd, then she nodded at me and shouted to one of her employees, "Alice, can you watch the front?"

Myrna pulled me to the side, out of earshot of the workers and customers. "What's up?"

"Well, you probably heard Lavinia was found dead this morning," I said tentatively. There was no love lost between Myrna and Lavinia and I wasn't sure what her reaction would be.

"Darned old fool fell down the steps, I hear."

"Maybe…"

She looked over her blue framed cats-eye glasses at me, her brow wrinkling in confusion. "What are you saying—she didn't fall?"

"It's possible she had some help."

Myrna snorted. "Well, I know a few people that would have liked to help, but I thought the police were ruling it an accident."

"They are. It probably was. But I was just wondering if you saw anyone around this morning. I know you open up early, and it looks like Lavinia went in early for some reason, so I was wondering if someone else was in there."

Myrna crossed her arms over her ample breasts, scrunched up her face and tapped the pencil on her lips. "Let me think … I came in to set things up early—you know we get an early morning coffee crowd—so I spent most of my time out back."

"Oh, so you didn't see anyone or anything out of the ordinary?"

"Well, now come to think of it, I did. I took the trash out to the dumpster in the alley. The church is right at the end of the alley and I happened to glance down and saw that woman that runs the new real estate business."

"Ophelia Withington?" I asked. Ophelia had come to town about ten years ago and opened a real estate business. She was hardly 'new', but these Yankee old-timers considered anyone not born here to be 'new'. Ophelia had married auctioneer Pete Withington, who had passed away a couple of years ago.

"Yeah, that's her. I thought it was strange that she'd be out that early in the morning and even stranger what she was wearing," Myrna said.

"Why? What was she wearing?"

Myrna looked at me with a funny look on her face. "She was wearing one of them big old raincoats ... a trench coat, I think they're called. I can't imagine why she'd want to traipse around in that thing. Heck, they weren't even forecasting rain."

Chapter Four

I couldn't wait to interrogate Ophelia, so I grabbed my sandwich and raced to my old Jeep Cherokee in the parking lot. The bookstore wouldn't suffer too much if I kept it closed for a few hours over lunch.

The day had warmed to an invigorating seventy degrees. The fresh mountain air gave me a burst of energy as I pulled out onto Main Street. I drove past the early 1900s storefronts. Some were brick, some clapboard, but all had been recently renovated so as to keep the nostalgia of the town's past while looking neat as a pin.

Withington Real Estate wasn't much more than a mile's drive. I munched on my sandwich as I drove, enjoying the mountain vista view revealed by the steep drop to the left. On the right, the stark granite face of the mountain jutted up into the sky.

I pulled up in front of my destination just as I swallowed the last of my sandwich. The building was an old colonial Ophelia had purchased and retrofitted into office space. I recognized her Beamer in the parking lot.

Brushing the crumbs off my lap, I trotted up to the door and opened it, revealing the wide pine flooring of the reception area that used to be the living room of the house.

An antique oak desk sat at one end of the room. Comfortable looking upholstered chairs and a sofa sat along the walls. It almost looked like a regular living room, except for the receptionist sitting behind the desk.

I approached the young girl. She couldn't have been more than twenty, but the way she caked on the makeup made her look older.

"Can I help you?" she asked through bright red lips.

"I was hoping to talk to Ophelia."

The girl looked at me uncertainly and I got the impression she was about to give me the brush-off, so I said, "Tell her it's Wilhelmina Chance. I know she'll want to talk to me."

I knew Ophelia would want to talk to me because she'd been pestering me to sell my grandmother's thirty-five-hundred square foot Victorian on twenty acres since I'd inherited it. If she got the impression that's why I was here, it certainly wasn't my fault.

The receptionist picked up the phone, told Ophelia I was there and replaced the receiver, then stood up. "This way, please."

She scooted out from behind the desk and I followed her down the hall. I couldn't help but notice her skirt was a bit too short, but if I still had legs like hers I'd probably wear one that short, too. Not that my legs were *that* bad, especially for pushing fifty. I exercised a lot and was still slim, but they were scarred up from the accident and I didn't like to show them off anymore.

Ophelia met us at the door of a bright blue and yellow room that boasted a tasteful, marble-mantled fireplace. Her frosted blonde hair was perfectly coiffed and a strand of creamy white pearls hung around her neck, the only accent to her tasteful beige and black dress.

I pushed my frizzy red curls into place self-consciously.

"Wilhelmina; how nice to see you." Ophelia held out her hand and I got a whiff of Chanel No. 5. Although her voice sounded pleasant, her dark eyes bore into me with a predatory glare. It was clear to me that Ophelia was interested in only one thing—getting big commissions from selling houses.

"Same here," I lied as I shook her hand.

She gestured toward a chair and I sank down into the tufted leather while she went back around to the other side of her desk.

"So, what brings you here?" Her brows raised in hopeful arcs. "Did you finally decide to sell? That property is so much for a single woman to manage."

"It is, but that's not why I'm here," I said, ignoring her obvious disappointment. "I'm sure you've heard that Lavinia was found dead at the library this morning."

"Yes, such sad news." Ophelia's face showed no emotion.

"Well, I heard you were there this morning and I wondered if you saw anything."

Ophelia's back stiffened. "Me? I wasn't at the library. And why are you asking about it? I heard she slipped and fell."

"Oh, she did," I said to soothe her and put her off guard, afraid she might clam up if she thought I was accusing her. "It's just that Lavinia was in there earlier than usual and I was wondering if someone else was there, too. Someone said they saw you near the church right down the street. I was wondering if you noticed anything unusual or saw anyone."

Ophelia's eyes darted around the room, her mouth set in a firm line. "Who told you they saw me?"

"I'd rather not say. What were you doing there that early anyway?"

"Well, I'd say that's none of your business," she huffed. "But if you must know I was ... err ... lighting a candle in memory of Pete."

She placed her palms on the desk and pushed up from her chair. I noticed she still wore her wedding rings—a large diamond and wide gold band that blinked in the sunlight.

"So you didn't see anything strange or notice anyone at the library? Did you see Lavinia?"

"No. No. And no." She came around the desk and opened the door, inviting me to leave.

I can take a hint, so I stood. "Okay, let me know if you remember anything. Sorry to bother you."

I felt her eyes drill into my back as I walked down the hall, through the reception area and out the door.

A niggle of doubt tickled my stomach as I got into my car. I was almost certain Ophelia was being evasive. Lavinia had said she was lighting a candle at almost the same time—wouldn't Ophelia have seen her? It *was* possible they had missed each other. I wasn't sure of the exact timing.

I doubted Ophelia had pushed Lavinia—what would be her motive? But if she wasn't being evasive because she knew something about Lavinia's murder, then what, exactly, was she hiding?

***

"Ophelia Withington?" Pepper scrunched up her nose. "I don't think she's the killer."

35

"Why not?" I asked. "Maybe she had some kind of grudge against Lavinia. She does seem to be mean, selfish and spiteful."

"She wasn't always that way, you know." Pepper sat down on the sofa while she waited for me to organize my sales receipts for the day.

"Really?" I cocked my head at her.

"She was actually very nice and kind when she first came here. Pete's lengthy illness and death made her bitter." Pepper looked at the canister of tea leaves she'd brought from her store. "Come to think of it, she might benefit from one of my teas."

My brows shot up. Pepper's special tea's sometimes backfired—I shuddered to think of Ophelia Withington being even meaner than she was now.

I took a sip from the tall glass of iced tea Pepper had brought. She usually closed up the tea room earlier than I closed the bookstore. Sometimes she'd bring a snack or tea over, which we'd enjoy before we walked down to our cars together. Today she'd brought iced tea to celebrate the beginning of spring—it was only sixty outside, but after a long winter in the White Mountains, sixty felt like summer.

I finished my record keeping and pushed the drawer of my antique cash register shut.

"All finished?" Pepper asked. "Looks like you made some sales today."

"I had a pretty good day. Sold a mint condition, first edition of Nancy Drew and made a few sales from the used book section." The Nancy Drew made me a couple thousand richer—the used books would buy me coffee for the week.

"That's great," Pepper said. "I had a visit from Derek Bates. He wanted some Wolfsbane tea. He's such a nice guy."

"He is. He came here, too. He was looking for an old family scrapbook. I guess his mother sold it at a yard sale by mistake."

Pepper burst out laughing. The Bates family came from old money. Actually more like old-old money. So old that no one remembered how they originally made the money.

"Idris let her have a yard sale? I can't imagine that."

"Me, either." I smiled as I pictured the look of delight on the faces of local antique dealers when they saw yard sale tables loaded up with antiques spread all over the lawn of the gigantic stone mansion just outside town.

"Felicity must have snuck in a sale while Idris was away."

"I hear the old guy is pretty tight-fisted with the money."

"Yep, he sure is." Pepper nodded. "He controls the money Felicity inherited from Derek and Carson's father with an iron fist. He lets her and the boys live in the mansion like they did when his son was alive, but doesn't give her much else to live on. Rumor has it she's been selling stuff off secretly for years."

"I feel sorry Derek and Carson … dependent on Idris for money. Of course, they could just go out and get jobs and gain their own independence." I grabbed my key and started for the door. "You ready?"

Pepper stood up. "So, what are you going to do about Ophelia?"

I pressed my lips together as we walked toward the door. "I'm not sure. I guess I need to do more checking. Myrna saw her near the library this morning and she was wearing a bulky coat. It might have looked like a cape in the shadow Lavinia described." I remembered the sunlight glinting off Ophelia's ring. "And she wears a wide ring. Not exactly the kind Lavinia thought she saw, but maybe she wasn't accurate on that. I mean, she only saw it as she was being pushed down the stairs."

"But *why* would she want to kill Lavinia?"

Pandora let out a wail and we both turned to look at the cat, who was sitting by the very spot I'd last seen Lavinia's ghost.

"I guess that's what I need to find out."

Chapter Five

I pulled my Jeep into the long driveway that led to the one hundred fifty year old Victorian I'd inherited from my grandmother. My heart warmed at the sight of the house that held so many wonderful childhood memories.

It was a large house, painted white with black shutters, and consisted of three stories with two living rooms and four or five bedrooms, depending on how you looked at it. The front boasted turrets on either side. Those turret rooms with their rounded walls were my favorite. The house was too big for one person, but I loved it and couldn't imagine ever selling.

I parked at the end of the driveway on the side of the house, just short of the red with white-trim barn. The barn was almost as big as the house and had been home to five horses at one time. The inside still smelled of old leather saddles, hay and manure. The stalls bore teeth marks where the horses had chewed the wood. I loved going in there. Sometimes I could almost hear the horses whinny. I fancied I might get one myself someday.

I opened the car door and Pandora shot across my lap and ran onto the porch on the side of the house. Looking back at me, she meowed impatiently as I limped up the porch steps—it had been a long day and my leg was starting to hurt.

The porch led straight to the kitchen and Pandora didn't waste any time getting over to her food bowl.

"Meow!" She paced back and forth, rubbing her face on the whitewashed country cabinets.

I pressed the button on my answering machine, then opened the cabinet and pulled out a bag of cat food. I had a cell phone like most people, but still preferred people to leave messages on my home phone. I guess I was kind of old-fashioned and didn't really like being all that accessible or being interrupted at all hours of the day on my cell.

"Willa, it's Barry. Just wanted to let you know I picked up a box of books in my travels for you. Let me know when we can get together—*Beep*."

Barry was one of the local antique dealers. Most of the antique dealers in the area had a good working relationship. If one of us was at an auction or yard sale and saw something that we thought another dealer would be interested in selling for a ridiculously low price, we'd pick it up for them. Last summer, I'd purchased a set of sterling silver Tiffany nut dishes at a yard sale for Barry for only a dollar. He'd made a bundle on them and I'd gotten a steak dinner as a 'thank you'.

"I wonder if there will be a treasure in that box of books," I said to Pandora as I bent down to fill her dish.

Something in the living room caught my eye. A greenish glow. I realized it was the round crystal paperweight my elderly neighbor, Elspeth Whipple, had given me as a 'moving-in' gift. From my bent-over position, I must have been looking at the paperweight at just the right angle to catch the reflection of light.

The paperweight was beautiful—a large, clear orb that reflected prisms of light almost magically. Elspeth had presented it to me the day I'd moved in and said I should keep it handy as I might find it very useful. I guess she didn't realize everything was done digitally now and I wouldn't have much paper that I needed to weigh down. Still, I kept it displayed prominently on my coffee table just for its beauty and sentiment.

Which reminded me—I should go over and check on Elspeth before supper. She was as old as the hills and had been Gram's neighbor forever. They'd been close and Gram had even put a note with her will asking me to check on Elspeth frequently.

I pulled my jean jacket off the peg by the kitchen door and shoved my feet into black rubber boots. The temperature was already falling from the high of the day and it would be chilly by the time I made my way back from Elspeth's house. Slipping out the back door, I heard the familiar slap of the cat door flapping as Pandora bolted out behind me. She was never one to miss a trip over to see Elspeth or her cats.

Elspeth lived one street over, but there was a shortcut through the woods. Clumps of winter snow were still visible under the trees, but the main trail was nearly bare. I walked the path, focusing on the drier spots and trying not to slip in the layers of wet leaves that carpeted the path. My leg was still weak and slipping wouldn't do it any good. Chickadee's, sparrows and nuthatches chirped their last songs of the day as they flitted between the bare branches of the trees. I noticed the unmistakable impressions of deer tracks and I reminded myself to put out some apples and carrots.

I bit my lip as I considered how to tell Elspeth about Lavinia—I didn't want her to be shocked. Not that she was frail or anything, she was actually quite feisty and in excellent health. Still I wanted to make sure to break the news in the most gentle way. I didn't want her finding out about it through the Mystic Notch grapevine—better for me to tell her and be able to comfort her and calm any fears she might have.

The trees were still bare of leaves and it wasn't long before I could see Elspeth's green and pink house through the branches. It was a cute, turn-of-the-century cottage with a wraparound porch and intricate gingerbread molding all along the roofline.

The porch posts were covered with thorny vines that would burst with fragrant pink roses in summer. I walked up and tapped on the door.

Elspeth answered within seconds. Her face was flushed under snow-white hair that was woven into a thick braid on top of her head. She wiped her hands on her blue toile apron.

"Hi Willa. I was just in the kitchen." Elspeth held the door wide open. "Come on in."

Pandora pushed in ahead of me, greeting the orange striped tomcat that always seemed to be weaving its way around Elspeth's ankles with a catty meow. Two more cats came running from the hallway, a fluffy Maine Coon and a regal Siamese. Elspeth had quite a collection of cats—I wasn't sure exactly how many, but I was pretty sure it was more than the three I saw in front of me. We headed toward the kitchen while the cats went through their usual sniffing ritual.

As I entered Elspeth's old-fashioned kitchen, my eyes were immediately drawn to the two pies on the counter. They looked fresh from the oven. The steam rising out of their fork pricked middles spiced the room with the scent of vanilla, sugar and cinnamon.

"I just came by to see if you needed anything," I said.

"Oh, thank you, dear. I don't need anything." She gestured toward the pies and my mouth started to water as I noticed the apple filling bubbling up through the slits in the golden brown crust. "I was just putting up these pies. One is for you."

"For me?"

"Yes, I had an idea you'd be stopping by tonight." She studied me, her light blue eyes tinged with concern. "You look a little wan, dear ... did something happen today?"

I frowned. How did she always seem to know these things?

"Well, as a matter of fact, something did happen downtown today," I said as Elspeth started packing up one of the pies. "Lavinia had an accident at the library."

"An accident? Oh, I do hope she's okay."

"Well, I'm sorry to say she's ... umm ... passed."

Elspeth whirled around to look at me. "Dead? At the library? What happened?"

"She fell down the stairs."

Elspeth's eyes narrowed. "Fell? That doesn't seem like Lavinia. She was pretty careful where she stepped, especially since she got the cane."

"I found her at the bottom of the stairs in the back. I guess she must have slipped. Her cane was lying at the top of the stairs." I left out the part about the blood.

"So, you don't suspect foul play?"

My stomach tightened. Funny she should ask. I certainly wasn't going to tell her that I talked to ghosts, so I simply said, "We don't think so."

"Is Augusta investigating it, or did she simply rule it as an accident?"

"I'm not sure if she's made a final decision on it yet." I made a mental note to call Augusta and find out if they'd gotten autopsy results and made a ruling.

"Oh, dear." Elspeth turned back to the pies. "That *is* disturbing."

"Sorry to bring bad news. I hope you're not too upset."

"Oh, no. I'm fine." Elspeth handed me the pie, nicely packed in a Tupperware carrier and inside a cloth bag with a carrying strap.

"Thanks. I guess I'd better get home, then."

Elspeth followed me down the hall and opened the door for me.

I stepped out onto the porch, then turned back to her. "Don't forget, if you need anything, just give me a call—I'm only across the woods, just a hop, skip and a jump away."

"Yes, dear," she said. As I made my way down the steps, she added, "Oh, and Willa?"

I half turned and looked at her over my shoulder. "Yes ...?"

"You be careful now ... there may be danger about."

Chapter Six

Pandora's whiskers twitched as she watched Willa and Elspeth disappear into the kitchen before following the orange tomcat, Tigger, out the cat door to the small barn where the cats usually gathered.

Pandora trotted into the barn behind Tigger. Nine sets of eyes blinked at them in the dark.

"I figured you'd show up eventually," Otis, the fat calico's sarcastic voice rang down from atop a tall bale of hay.

Pandora felt the hairs on her back prickle. She got along well with all the others of her kind, but Otis had been a thorn in her side since the beginning. He was one of the old ones ... an ancient feline that had served many humans. Pandora was a newer soul, with new ideas. For some reason, Otis felt threatened by these ideas.

Pandora arched her back and hissed at the calico.

"Now stop it, you two." Kelley, the Maine Coon swiped her paw in the air between them.

"So, you heard about the trouble brewing from the other side," Snowball, the fluffy white Persian, purred as she licked her paw.

"Lavinia came to the bookstore and verified her death was no accident," Pandora started, then paused for attention. She was one of the few cats that could talk to the other side. All eyes were on her and she savored the moment before continuing. "She didn't see who did it, though."

The others heaved a collective sigh.

"So, the evil ones have spilled first blood." The deep baritone of Inkspot, the twenty-two pound black cat rang out from the back of the barn.

"Do you always have to be so dramatic?" Snowball hissed at him.

Inkspot trotted toward the other cats that had formed a small circle in the middle of the barn and stood in front of Pandora.

"Is it not true?" he asked.

Pandora wrinkled her pink nose, remembering the noxious coppery smell of blood in the library. Her senses, many times more sensitive than humans, could smell it even out on the street that morning.

"Well, there was a lot of blood ..." she said.

"I think he was talking metaphorically, you know, trying to show off," Snowball said.

Sasha, the sleek Siamese jumped into the middle of the circle. "Let's not argue. We need to help our humans any way we can."

Pandora sat on her haunches and licked her paw. They were an elite species of cats sworn to

48

help humans since ancient times—a task made more difficult by the fact that humans simply didn't have the feline's superior methods of communication. Some of them could learn, but others never did.

Pandora flicked her paw behind her ear as she thought about Willa, her human. She'd been with Willa's grandmother, Anna, since the beginning.

Anna had understood her.

Willa, on the other hand, obviously had no idea what Pandora was trying to tell her. Pandora missed Anna terribly, but she was starting to develop a small liking to her new human—even though Willa was rather skinny and her lap not nearly as comfortable as Anna's.

She didn't yet have the rapport with Willa that she'd developed with Anna, but it had taken years to get to that point with the grandmother, so there was still hope. Though that didn't help her much now ... and it seemed that right now, communicating with her human was critical.

Pandora narrowed her eyes. "How can we help them?"

"We must make sure the evil ones do not gain ground," Inkspot said in his usual vague manner.

"Anyone got an idea on how to do that?" Sasha's luminous blue eyes scanned the crowd.

"Only true magic can stop them for good," Otis spoke from his perch on top of the hay. "But it's not time for that. The best we can do is to guide the humans to slow down the evil ones."

"And how do we do that?" Pandora asked.

"By helping them find the killer before he gets what he wants," Otis replied.

"But how can we help them if we don't even know who the killer is?" Sasha asked.

A small cat padded into the middle of the circle. Her name was Truffles and she was a Tortoiseshell, predominantly black with orange mottling. Her large, greenish-yellow eyes glowed with excitement. "I think I know how."

"You?" Inkspot turned his green eyes on the small cat. "Have you been talking to the wild ones again?"

The wild ones were the feral cats of Mystic Notch. They served no humans and lived on the streets of town and in the forests, surviving on scraps and taking shelter as they could. They had eyes everywhere and knew much about what was going on in Mystic Notch.

"The wild ones found something." Truffles turned with a flick of her tail and headed toward the door. "Follow me, and I'll take you to it. I think it might help reveal the killer."

Chapter Seven

I traipsed back through the woods toward my house, feeling the absence of Pandora at my side. She hadn't been in Elspeth's house when I left and I didn't see her outside.

Where was she? I glanced back over my shoulder as I pulled my cell phone out to call Augusta.

"Pandora!" I yelled. Was I expecting her to come bounding through the woods? She'd never come when I called before.

I felt a stab of worry for the cat—I had to admit, I was getting kind of attached to the fur ball even though she did act strangely at times.

I waited a few seconds, then turned with a shrug. It would be dark soon and I didn't want to be in the woods after sunset. Pandora would find her way home—she always did.

I pulled Augusta up on my contacts list and pressed the button. She answered on the first ring.

"Hey, Willa. What's up?" Her voice was muffled like she had a jelly donut stuffed in her mouth.

"Are you eating?" I asked.

"Yep. Chocolate cruller." Not a jelly donut, but I was close. I wondered how she could eat so many donuts and still not gain an ounce.

"I was just calling to see if there was anything new about Lavinia. Do you have any idea why she was in the library that early?" I asked.

Augusta paused. I could hear her swallow the cruller. "You know I'm not supposed to talk about ongoing cases."

"Oh, so it is still open?" My house came into view in the distance and I picked up the pace.

Augusta laughed. "I guess I can tell you that I have some doubts. I can't just write it off if I have a doubt, so I sent the body from Stilton's to the medical examiner."

"Ahh ... so you *do* suspect foul play." I said it as more of a statement than a question.

"Not necessarily. But I have a funny feeling and my duty is to err on the side of caution."

Augusta often had 'funny feelings' about cases and they usually turned out to be quite accurate. She was a natural cop, with good intuition.

"Okay. Well, let me know what you find out," I said as I jogged up the farmers porch steps and opened my back door.

"Will do." Augusta said. "Hey, wait a minute. Why are you so interested?"

"Oh, no reason, really." I stepped into the back entry, the back stairs were in front of me, the kitchen to my right and a small area for boots and coats to the left. I turned to the left, placed the bag with the pie on the floor and slid my left boot off with my right toe. "It's just that I found her, so I kind of feel like I want closure or something."

"I hope that's all it is, Willa," Augusta warned. "I don't want you going off on some wild investigation."

"Who, me?" I asked as I slid my right boot off. "Never."

Augusta laughed. "Okay, just be careful, then."

"I will." I snapped the phone shut and shrugged out of my coat, hanging it on the hook.

"So you didn't find my killer yet?"

I whirled around, my heart seizing in my chest. The cell phone slipped from my hand and clattered to the floor.

Lavinia's ghost sat at the oak claw-foot kitchen table, her hands folded in front of her as if she were waiting for me to serve tea.

"Lavinia! You scared the crap out of me."

"Sorry, dear. I just wanted to catch up and see if you'd made any progress."

I blew out a puff of air, picked the bag with the pie up and headed toward the fridge. On the way, I grabbed a tube of *Iced Fire* out of the basket I kept handy on the kitchen island. My leg was starting to hurt and I needed something to ease the pain.

"Myrna saw Ophelia Withington in town that morning." I put the pie in the fridge, then sat across from Lavinia, pulling the chair next to me closer so I could rest my leg on it.

Lavinia pressed her ghostly lips together. "That woman! I wouldn't put it past her to push me down the stairs."

I raised my brow at her as I eased up the leg of my jeans. "You didn't get along?"

"Not one bit. Oh, she was fine when she first came to town, but after Pete died she turned into a miserable witch trying to make everyone else around her just as bitter as she was."

"So you think she did it? But why? Why would she be in the library?" I opened the tube of *Iced Fire* and rolled some of it onto my leg, the medicinal peppermint smell tickling my nose.

"I'm not sure ... unless ..." Lavinia's voice trailed off.

"Unless, what?" I massaged my leg, the ache starting to disappear as the sensation of cold and hot from the *Iced Fire* worked its way into the muscle.

"No, I can't say." Lavinia shook her head. "Anyway she wouldn't have any reason to be in the library. She'd already scoured it."

"Scoured it? For what?"

"Oh, that's not important. It has nothing to do with my murder," Lavinia said, pushing herself up from the table. "You keep looking, and please do be careful. There may be danger about."

And with that, Lavinia disappeared, leaving me staring at the empty chair across the table from me.

Her parting words caused a chill to run up my spine ... Elspeth had said almost the same exact thing to me.

Shaking my head, I stood up. I was getting creeped out for nothing. A good, hot bath would fix that and make my leg almost as good as new. I tossed the *Iced Fire* into the basket and walked through the living room to the front stairs.

A sound made me pause at the foot of the stairs. Was that the flap of the cat door? Peeking back over my shoulder into the living room, I strained my ears, listening for the sound of Pandora's paws or her subtle meow. My heart hitched as I realized it had only been my imagination—Pandora was still outside.

I turned back to the stairs with a sigh. Pandora had been taking care of herself long before I came along and she certainly could take care of herself without me worrying about her, I thought, as I ascended the stairs.

Below me in the living room, the paperweight lit with an eerie glow. If I'd noticed, and cared to investigate further, I would have seen Pandora running through the streets of downtown Mystic Notch deep inside the globe.

But I didn't notice, so I went ahead with my bath and climbed into bed with a good book, never knowing that my furry feline friend was running around in the night, miles from home.

Chapter Eight

Pandora must have returned sometime during the night because I woke up with her tail flicking me in the face as she sat on my chest, kneading my bladder. She really knew how to wake a girl up.

I pushed her off, but not too hard. Truth be told, I was relieved she was safe. I sat up and pulled her onto my lap, scratching her behind the ears. She rewarded me with a few seconds of purring before wriggling out of my arms and running downstairs.

I used the bathroom, took a quick shower and threw on jeans and a sweatshirt before trotting downstairs where I fed Pandora and myself a quick breakfast. Fancy Feast for her—Corn Flakes for me.

We got to the bookstore late again and I was just turning the sign to 'Open' when Hattie, Cordelia, Bing and Josiah filed in through the door.

Bing handed me a Styrofoam cup filled with coffee just as my cell phone made a noise.

"Damn, I thought I shut this thing off." I pulled it out of my pocket. The display showed a text from another antique dealer friend, Maggie.

Picked up a box of old books for you.

"More books?" I said to myself as I shut off the phone.

"What's that about books?" Bing looked at me curiously.

"Oh, nothing. Maggie picked up a box of old books for me."

"Where?" he asked. Maggie had grown up in Mystic Notch and Bing had known her since she was a kid, just like he'd known me since I was a kid.

I frowned at him. What was he so interested in that for? "Umm... I have no idea. We do that for each other sometimes—you know—if we see something cheap enough that the other might be interested in. Barry has a box for me, too. Remember last summer when I gave him those nut dishes from the yard sale?"

"Oh, right. Of course." He shrugged, and then took a pack of cards out of his shirt pocket and joined the others who were already lounging on the couch. "So, did you find out any more about why Lavinia was in the library?"

"Not really," I muttered. It didn't seem fair to mention Myrna had seen Ophelia that morning until I knew exactly what she was up to and I sure as heck couldn't tell them that Lavinia's ghost had told me her death was no accident.

Bing raised a bushy eyebrow at me as he made a card disappear in thin air, then made a show of retrieving it from his sock.

"We checked in the Gazette and there was no notice of a book sale at the library," Hattie said as she sipped her tea.

"But she could have come in early for another reason," Josiah said.

"Right," I offered. "There are probably lots of reasons she could have come in early."

Cordelia bit her lower lip. "I never knew her to come in early, Josiah."

"Well, something brought her there," Bing said.

Hattie shrugged. "I guess it really doesn't matter. It was an accident, right?"

Everyone looked at me and I felt like a deer trapped in the headlights. Thankfully, I was saved by Pandora, who let out an ungodly wail from the other end of the bookstore just before something landed on the floor with a loud crash.

"What the heck?" I sprinted toward the source of the noise and found Pandora sitting in the mystery aisle amidst a pile of books.

"Did you knock these down?"

"Mew."

"That's not nice." I stooped and picked up the books, putting them back on the shelf while she watched with her golden green eyes.

I stood and pointed my finger at her. "Don't do that again."

She gave me a bored look and started washing her face.

"Is everything okay?" Cordelia yelled.

"Yep. Pandora just knocked some books down." I walked back to the front, picking my coffee up from the counter where I'd left it.

"So, anyway, we were saying that Lavinia's unfortunate accident was just that." Bing slid his eyes over to me. "That's what Augusta says, right?"

"That's what she thought when we were in the library, but you know how she is ... she won't say a word about an ongoing case to me." I crossed my fingers behind my back. It wasn't exactly a lie. She really didn't like to talk about cases. I was sure she wouldn't want me repeating her doubts to everyone in town.

"All this talk is making me depressed," Hattie said. "I think I need to visit the chocolate store."

"Me, too!" Cordelia jumped up from her seat.

Josiah drained his coffee cup. "Yep, guess I better get going and let you do your work."

The four of them made their way out the door. Bing was last and he held back for a second, half-closing the door, then turning to look at me.

I'd busied myself with some work behind the counter, but sensed him looking and glanced over at him, my brows creeping up my forehead.

"Willa … it might be best if you didn't dig into this whole thing with Lavinia. It could be dangerous," Bing said, ducking out the door before I had a chance to answer him.

I stared at the door. Was that a warning … or a threat? I couldn't tell by his tone or the look on his face and I didn't have much time to think about it because just then I heard another crash and Pandora's wail.

I ran to the back of the store. Pandora sat amidst a pile of books … again. The same darn books.

"Really?" I bent down to put the books back. "What is wrong with you?"

Nothing. I'm trying to give you a clue. Her meows almost sounded like words as I put the books back in their place.

"Now, no messing with these books again." I tapped my finger on her pink nose.

She looked at me defiantly, reached out her paw and pulled a book off the shelf.

I rolled my eyes. "Cut that out!" I picked up the book and shoved it back into its spot.

"Mew!" She pulled it out again.

I felt my temper starting to rise. What was up with her? I glanced at the title as I picked up the book to put it back, yet again. *Murder Weapon Mayhem.* How appropriate, given what was going on with Lavinia.

I slid the book back in place.

"Wait a minute ... murder ... weapon." I looked at Pandora, who stared at me expectantly.

"Of course!" I snapped my fingers and stood up. "Why didn't I think of that before? Lavinia said she was whacked on the back of the head, which means that somewhere out there is a murder weapon that might have a clue to the murderer ... all we have to do is find it."

***

The rest of the day was uneventful. I spent most of it trying to decide where to search for the murder weapon. As the day drew on, doubt bloomed in my gut. The warnings I'd had from three people—well, two people and a ghost—echoed in my head.

It could be dangerous to look for the murder weapon on my own, but I couldn't very well tell Augusta I knew someone had clonked Lavinia on the back of the head.

It was up to me to find the murder weapon. I wasn't sure how I'd explain finding it to Augusta, but I was sure I would come up with something.

Of course, if I knew what I was looking for, it would make it a lot easier to find. Something heavy that one could easily use to whack someone else on the back of the head with.

I figured the best place to start was the library, so I closed up shop at five and headed down the street with Pandora following me ... well, I should say in front of me. The cat had the strangest way of following me by walking ahead of me. I had no idea how she knew where I was going, but somehow she did.

I thought back to the morning I'd found Lavinia. Impossible to believe it was just yesterday, but it was. She hadn't been dead long when I'd found her, so that meant the killer had to make his—or her—escape through town in the morning hours. If I were a killer, I'd want to ditch that murder weapon as fast as I could, which is why I figured it would be somewhere near the library.

As I stared at the gothic stone building, I realized the killer wouldn't have come back out the front. There were too many people around on Maine Street.

"Meow." Pandora peeked out from the side of the library, then turned, her tail flicking like a finger beckoning me to follow her.

"Good idea, Pandora." The killer would have gone out the only other door, which was in the back. I followed her around the corner of the library. I'd never been behind the building before and was surprised that the area behind it was so small. It was paved, and there was a dumpster that I hoped I wouldn't have to jump inside of to find what I was looking for.

I chose to look everywhere else first. I walked around the edge of the pavement and looked in the corners of the building. I was squatting down, the side of my head almost on the ground so that I could peer under the dumpster, when I heard a low, guttural animal sound coming from behind me.

The hairs on the back of my neck stood up and I jerked my head around to see Pandora, her back arched, having a stare down with another cat. The other cat was a raggedy looking ginger-colored thing with wild yellow eyes. Three other cats stood about five feet away behind it.

I'd heard there was a feral cat colony around here and I guessed these cats were part of it. I noticed a small black and white kitten that couldn't have been more than six months old with a torn-up ear and my heart tugged. They looked well-fed, though, and I wondered briefly how they found shelter and what they ate.

I stood motionless, not knowing exactly what to do. Pandora and the other cat must have come to some sort of agreement, because they stopped making their noises and the other cat and his minions backed up.

Pandora trotted off after them and I could just barely make out a trail into the woods. The train tracks were back there somewhere—it would be a perfect get-away route for the killer! The tracks wandered behind several buildings then crossed Main Street at the other end of town. The killer could have run down them, then popped back out onto the street as if he had never been near the library.

I rushed in after Pandora, scanning the ground for something that could be the murder weapon.

She stopped in front of me and that's when I saw it.

It had been thrown off to the side and was half-buried in the leaves, but I recognized the part of it that was sticking up ... it was the heavy metal embosser Lavinia used to emboss the pages of the books with the library insignia. The library had three of them and, apparently, no one had noticed one was missing.

I stepped off the trail toward the embosser, bending down to get a better look. Yep, that was definitely the library's embosser. A thread of navy blue fabric caught on one of the screws flapped in the wind ... and was that blood on the side?

My heart thudded in my chest as I reached out to pick it up ...

"Stop right there! Put your hands in the air, stand up slowly and turn around!"

Chapter Nine

A steely gray glare coming from the broad shouldered behemoth who was holding the gun on me rooted me to the spot. Adrenalin shot through my body as my mind registered a chiseled jaw, trim waist and sheriff's uniform.

Sheriff's uniform?

Augusta was the sheriff here, and this guy sure as heck wasn't Augusta.

"Who the hell are you?" I probably should have asked more nicely, but I was mad ... and a little scared.

His left eyebrow quirked up and I thought I saw a smile tease the corners of his lips.

"I might ask you the same," he said, his eyes shifting to the embosser still lying on the ground. "What are you doing here and what is that you were bending over?"

Panic lapped at my stomach as I considered how to explain exactly what I was doing there. I certainly couldn't tell him I was looking for the murder weapon since I wasn't supposed to know there even *was* a murder.

"Meow!"

I shot the cat a grateful look. "My cat ... I was here looking for my cat."

As if on cue, Pandora trotted over to my side and rubbed her face against my leg.

Relief washed away the panic as a familiar figure came around the corner—Augusta.

"Willa? What's going on here?" Augusta looked from the behemoth to me, her brow wrinkled in confusion.

"You know her?" Behemoth asked.

Augusta sighed and holstered her gun. "You can put your gun away, Striker. It's my sister."

"Who the hell is *he*?" I asked Augusta, gesturing toward Striker with my chin. I still had my hands up because the behemoth was still pointing his gun at me.

"This is Eddie Striker." Augusta nodded toward Striker. "He's the sheriff over in Dixford Pass. I asked him to help out since I don't have much experience with homicides."

"Homicide? So Lavinia *was* murdered." I tried to sound surprised.

Augusta shifted on her feet. "Yes, I suppose I can tell you since it's going to come out sooner or later. The medical examiner determined she was hit on the head with something. That probably didn't kill her, but it stunned her and the push down the stairs finished her off."

"Poor Lavinia," I said.

Augusta narrowed her eyes at me. "So, just what are *you* doing here behind the library?"

"What are *you* doing here?" I asked, wondering if they'd come to the same conclusion I had and were also looking for the murder weapon.

"I asked first," Augusta replied.

Striker was sliding his eyes back and forth between us, an amused expression on his face. I was not so amused that he still had his gun aimed at me.

"Pandora ran back here and I was trying to get her," I lied. Was I in store for some bad karma for lying to my sister? Probably.

"Are you sure that's all it is?" Augusta looked at me suspiciously. "I know how you have a habit of sticking your nose into investigations."

"Can I put my hands down?" My arms were starting to hurt, plus I wanted to avoid addressing Augusta's comment. It was true, I *did* have a habit of investigating on my own from my years of training as a crime journalist.

"Yes," Augusta sighed.

"No!" Striker shot Augusta a look.

I held my hands halfway up, my eyes wavering between the two of them.

"She could be a suspect. I caught her bending over that." Striker nodded toward the embosser.

"What is that?" Augusta walked over and bent down to inspect it.

"It's the embosser from the library. I saw it when I came back here after Pandora. I was going to pick it up and return it to the library when King Kong over here tried to shoot me down." Another lie ... bad karma was coming my way for sure.

Augusta took a plastic bag out of her pocket and deftly bagged the embosser without ever touching it with her fingers.

"Did you touch this?" She held the bag up in front of my face.

"No." At least I wasn't lying that time.

"Okay, I think we can let her go," Augusta held her hand up to squelch Striker's protest. "Striker, she's my sister. She found Lavinia and called it in."

"She found the body and now I catch her bending over the murder weapon? In Dixford Pass, she'd be my number one suspect," Striker said incredulously.

"I'll vouch for her. Let's take this to the lab. I think I see blood on the corner." Augusta turned to walk away and Striker reluctantly lowered his gun and followed. When they got to the corner of the building, Augusta half turned back toward me.

"Willa, you can put your hands down now," she shot over her shoulder. "Oh ... and don't leave town."

***

I walked to the parking lot, Pandora trotting at my side with a satisfied look on her face.

"Well, looks like we found the murder weapon," I said to her as I started the Jeep.

She ignored me, curled up in the passenger seat and went to sleep.

I thought about the murder weapon as I drove home. I couldn't really picture the perfectly-coiffed Ophelia smashing Lavinia on the back of the head with the embosser, but she was the only lead I had.

The embosser had blood on it. There was no doubt in my mind it was the murder weapon. I remembered the thread of navy blue fabric that was caught on one of the screws.

Was the fabric already on there or could it have come from the murderer?

Who else would have been in the library that morning and why? Did Lavinia have any enemies? Or was the intruder after something in the library, anyway? What would someone want in a library? All that was in there were books, and as far as I knew, none of them were valuable. Could there be something else of value in the library?

I pulled into my driveway and walked into the house like a zombie, exhausted from thinking.

As usual, Pandora sped ahead of me, making a beeline for her dish.

"Are you hungry?" I asked the obvious as I searched in the cupboard for her favorite food.

"You deserve a special treat, since you led me to the murder weapon."

I studied the cat as she ate. She *had* led me to the murder weapon, which was rather odd. But who was I to talk about odd? I talked to ghosts and that wasn't exactly normal.

I wished Lavinia's ghost would appear now. I had some questions for her. Maybe if I called her out?

"Lavinia?" I ventured.

No one appeared.

"Lavinia, I have some questions that might help solve your murder."

Still nothing. Darn ghosts, appear when you don't want them to and then they aren't around when you need them.

I opened the fridge to rummage for something to eat and spied Elspeth's apple pie—the perfect supper for a crazy day like today.

I cut an extra-large piece and topped it off with vanilla ice cream. Sitting at the table, I stretched my leg out on the chair and dug into the pie. The apples practically melted in my mouth, the sugar and cinnamon tantalizing my taste buds. The crust was perfectly crunchy and Elspeth had sprinkled it with large sugar crystals for an extra boost. The slightly melted ice cream added the perfect creamy complement.

I finished the pie and brought the plate to the sink, suddenly feeling exhausted. Limping up the stairs, I threw on pajamas and slid into bed with a good book about a pirate in 1820s England.

Pandora positioned herself at the foot of the bed. Her greenish-golden eyes glowed in the dark, watching me as I fell into a deep sleep.

In my dream, I was taken aboard a pirate ship against my will. Not that I minded, though ... the pirate looked kind of like Striker and I vaguely remember half-hoping he would ravish me like the pirate in my book had ravished the heroine. It was incredibly real and I slept deeply without moving a muscle.

So deeply, in fact, that I would never have noticed if someone snuck in and did a thorough search of my house and barn.

Chapter Ten

I got to the bookstore early the next day. Pandora settled into her cat bed in the window and I started sorting and putting away the books that had accumulated, which included a boxful from an internet auction I'd won and a pile of old books I'd picked up in my travels.

Inside the box was a wonderful set of five poetry books bound in rich brown leather with gold leaf on the edges of the pages. I carefully carried them to the poetry section and made room for them on the shelf at eye level.

"I shall tell you with a sigh, the poetry section needs some bulking up."

I gasped, momentarily startled at the voice in my ear, then turned to see the ghostly figure of Robert Frost at my side. The poet's ghost often hung around here in the poetry section where I had quite a collection of his books—he'd lived in New Hampshire while writing many of his poems, and his books were quite popular here.

I scanned the shelf critically. "You know what, Robert? You're right. These shelves are practically bare."

"Oh, and you could use some more historical books, too," a voice piped up several aisles down in the history section. I recognized the ghost as that of Franklin Pierce, the only US President from New Hampshire. He hung around here, too.

I had no idea why they choose to hang around in the bookstore, but they seemed like nice guys. At first, it was a little off-putting, but once I got used to them, I realized they could actually be good company ... except when they were arguing or being mischievous. You wouldn't expect it from such proper gentlemen, but I'd seen them run off giggling after knocking a book off a shelf in front of a customer, just to startle them.

Anyway, they were both right. I *did* need to get some fresh stock.

I remembered that both Barry and Maggie had called about books they'd picked up for me. I'd been so busy trying to find Lavinia's killer, I hadn't had time to go pick up the books. Well, I'd just have to make time.

"Did someone call me?" Lavinia materialized in the middle of the aisle.

"Sure, now you show up ... where were you when I was calling you at my house?"

Lavinia straightened, eyeing Robert and Franklin. "Well, now, we ghosts can't be at your beck and call, you know. There's lots to do on the other side."

"Are you going to introduce us?" Franklin raised a brow as he glided toward me.

"Where are your manners?" Robert asked.

I introduced them all and they swirled misty greetings to each other. I guess ghosts didn't just shake hands.

"Anyway, did you need something?" Lavinia asked.

"I was wondering if there was anyone who had a grudge against you. You know ... who might have wanted you ... dead."

"No one. I don't think it had anything to do with me," Lavinia said. "They were in the library before me. It must have been something in the library."

"You mean you were murdered?" Franklin's eyes widened. "My dear, how ... exciting."

"Yes, do tell us all about it." Robert drifted toward the end of the aisle and Lavinia followed, the three of them fading away as they chatted about Lavinia's murder.

"At least she won't be bugging me today," I said to Pandora as I unlocked the door and turned the shop sign to 'Open'.

Slipping back behind the counter, I set about examining the rest of the books. I was almost done when the bells over the door jingled. I looked up in time to see Hattie, Cordelia, Josiah and Bing come in, carrying the usual Styrofoam cups. Josiah had gotten mine this time and he pushed it across the counter toward me.

I flipped the plastic tab and took a sip, the bitter coffee warming my veins.

"Are you going to Lavinia's service tomorrow?" Hattie asked.

Lavinia materialized, peeking around the edge of one of the bookshelves, her ear cocked to hear the conversation.

"Yessuh," Josiah said. "I hear there's no viewing."

"Nope, the family didn't want it." Cordelia said. "Said they were being hounded enough by the press now that it's been deemed a murder."

"Did you know that, Willa?" Bing turned to me.

"I just found out," I said, watching Lavinia make motions of her nose growing like Pinocchio telling a lie.

"Is something wrong over there?" Hattie leaned forward in her seat, looking toward the spot where Lavinia was. Of course, she couldn't see her.

"No, I just noticed the books are out of order. I'll have to straighten them later," I said.

"Well, anyway, it's all over town about the murder," Hattie continued. "Who do you think did it?"

Yes, Willa. You're the crime journalist," Josiah cocked his head at me. "Who do *you* think did it?"

I shrugged. "I'm at a loss. You guys know the townspeople better than I. Do you have any idea who would want to hurt Lavinia?"

The four of them shook their heads.

"I don't."

"Can't think of a soul."

"Everyone liked Lavinia."

"Maybe it wasn't about Lavinia," Cordelia said. "Maybe she just got in the way."

Hattie frowned at her sister. "In the way of what?"

"Someone who wanted to take something from the library," Josiah said.

"But there's nothing, 'cept old books in there." Cordelia wrinkled up her face and turned to me. "None of those books have any value, do they?"

I shook my head. "Not that I know of."

"Not the books," Josiah said. "There are some valuable bronzes in there."

"Oh, you mean that bust of Franklin Pierce?" Cordelia asked.

"That one's not worth much. The real treasures are the ones by Frederick Remington."

"You mean the horse ones?" Hattie asked.

Josiah nodded. "Most people think they are replicas, but I'm pretty sure a few of those are originals. I remember back in sixty-five when Idris Bates donated them to the library. It was quite a to-do back then. 'Course, as the years have gone by, people have forgotten about them."

I looked at Josiah, open-mouthed. Although my area of expertise was antique books, I'd picked up enough information on general antiques to know that an original Remington bronze bust could be worth hundreds of thousands. Heck, even the good replicas are worth thousands.

"I don't remember ever noticing the busts in there," I said.

"Most people don't. Over the years they got shuffled around." Josiah turned to Bing. "Bing, you remember those don't you. I seem to recall even back then you had an interest in bronzes."

Bing nodded. "Now that you mention it, I do remember. I did have quite a collection of bronzes in my younger days, but I don't collect them anymore. Never had a Remington, though."

I remembered that Bing had an extensive collection of antiques, many of which he'd acquired from various parts of the world where he'd performed as a magician. He'd been collecting since he was a boy. When I was young, I used to love to go to his house and look at all the old stuff. He had a treasure trove of items stuffed in the attic, basement and barns. It was no surprise he'd collected a bronze or two in his day.

Josiah looked back at me. "You younger people wouldn't remember. They weren't worth nearly as much at the time they were donated, so no one paid much mind to what happened to them and they got moved downstairs."

Downstairs ... where Lavinia's body was found.

"Gosh, I had forgotten all about those," Cordelia said.

Hattie looked at the group solemnly. "Maybe someone else remembered about them and broke in to steal them."

"... And Lavinia stumbled across them and they killed her!" Cordelia added.

"Were any of the statues missing from the library?" Josiah asked me.

"I'm not sure, but you can bet I'm going to find out," I said.

"Well, then, I think I'll be on my way." Josiah pushed himself up from the couch. "I'll ask around about the bronzes and let you know if I come up with anything."

"Us, too," Cordelia and Hattie chorused, then gave each other a knuckle tap as they rose from the couch.

Bing got up with the others. I noticed he'd been unusually quiet.

"I wish you'd be careful if you are going to look into this, Willa," he said as he followed the others out the door. "There's a killer on the loose and now that the police are on it, it might be best to leave it to them."

"I'll be careful," I promised.

Bing looked like he was going to say something else, then he must have decided better of it as he turned and disappeared out the door.

Chapter Eleven

I finished sorting through the rest of the box, then left a message for Barry letting him know I'd be out to his place tomorrow to pick up the books he was holding for me. Maggie was in New York on a buying trip, so I'd have to wait until she got back to pick up the books from her.

It was a slow day, but between inventorying the new stock and putting the books on the shelf, I'd made a few sales, one of which was a book on US Presidents. I wondered how the buyer would feel if he knew Franklin Pierce was standing behind him nodding his approval as I rang up the sale.

I was taking a break in one of the purple chairs when the bells over the door jangled and Pepper came in, holding a tray of tea and finger sandwiches.

"It's slow over at the tea shop, so I left Camilla in charge and brought you some lunch." She set the tray on the table and sat beside me.

My stomach growled at the sight of the tiny sandwiches—thin white bread, cut into triangles with the crusts removed.

"Is that ham salad?" I asked as I reached for a sandwich.

"Yes, with pickles."

I loaded my plate with three of them, and poured some tea into the dainty china cup. Pepper had a collection of antique teacups that she used in her shop and this one had a thick gold lining inside and big yellow roses on the outside.

I poured some cream into the cup, glancing at her out of the corner of my eye. "You didn't put anything special in here, did you?"

Pepper laughed. "Nope. No special herbs in there, don't worry."

I bit into the sandwich, reveling in the burst of sweet ham and tangy pickle. "Nummy," I mumbled with my mouth full.

"So, did you find out any more about Lavinia's killer? I heard it's an official murder investigation now." Pepper settled back on the sofa, taking a teensy nibble from one of the molasses cookies stacked up on the tray.

I told her about the incident behind the library.

"Augusta must think this is serious if she called in Eddie Striker," Pepper said.

"You know him?"

"Of course." Pepper looked at me quizzically. "He grew up here. Don't you remember him from grade school?"

"Grade school?" I dug around in my memory, which to tell the truth wasn't that great anymore. I didn't remember any extra-large second grader named Eddie. "I don't remember."

"Anyway, he moved away to Dixford Pass when were about ten, I think. He went on to work for the CIA—super secret spy stuff, from what I hear. Then something happened and he came back to Dixford Pass to be the sheriff."

I pressed my lips together. "Well, I didn't like him very much ... he seemed like he wanted to shoot me."

"Was that because you acted less than hospitable to him?"

"Maybe," I laughed. I had been pretty hostile to him. "Anyway, I'm pretty sure that embosser is the murder weapon and I found something on it that might be a clue."

"What?'

"One of the screws that attached the seal to the handle was sticking out. There was a thread of navy blue fabric stuck on it. Like a thread that would have ripped off a coat ... or a cape."

"And you think that could have come from the murderer." Pepper said it as more of a statement than a question.

I nodded.

"So, now we need to find out who has a navy blue coat."

"Yes, I'd especially like to know if Ophelia has one. And there's something else..."

A movement at the shop door caught my eye and I glanced over to see something large blocking most of the light. I noticed a brown shirt and the ham salad spoiled in my stomach. "Please tell me that isn't—"

The door opened and in stepped Eddie Striker.

***

Striker paused just inside the doorway, his light gray eyes scanning the shop before he noticed us on the couch. Did I see his lips twitch upwards in a smile? I stared at the stone-faced look he was wearing and decided that must have been my imagination. Probably he just had indigestion or some kind of a strange twitch.

"Sheriff Striker, what a pleasant surprise," I said sarcastically. "What can I do for you?"

"Ms. Chance," he said, then frowned at Pepper.

"Hi, Eddie," Pepper cut in. "It's Pepper St. Onge ... from second grade."

"I thought you looked familiar." Striker shifted his weight from one foot to the other. "How are you?"

"Oh, great. Hey, would you like a sandwich?" Pepper gestured toward the tea tray and I almost laughed out loud picturing the tiny sandwich and teacup in Striker's large hands.

He frowned down at the tray and I figured he was probably thinking the same thing I was. I couldn't help but notice how his frown made the dimple on his cheek more prominent.

His face was slightly tanned, making his eyes look even lighter. His short-cropped dark hair had just a peppering of gray. I touched my own hair self-consciously, wondering why a little bit of gray always makes guys look more handsome, but just makes women look old. Not that I was noticing, but Sheriff Striker did look a lot more appealing now that he wasn't pointing a gun at me.

Striker looked up at me and our eyes met, sending a jolt through my heart. I was probably just scared he was going to arrest me. I ripped my eyes away from his in time to notice the bemused look on Pepper's face as she flicked her eyes from me to Striker and back again.

Striker cleared his throat. "Thanks, but I already ate lunch. I have some questions about what you found in the library the other day."

"Okay, fire away." I remained seated and rudely didn't invite him to join us.

Striker glanced at Pepper uncertainly.

"You can ask me in front of Pepper. She knows all about me finding Lavinia."

Pandora jumped down from her bed on the window and started sniffing around Striker's feet. He looked down at her, but didn't shoo her away.

"Where was the body when you found it?" he asked.

"Same place it was when Augusta came. I didn't touch it other than feeling for a pulse on her wrist."

"And you didn't notice anything out of the ordinary or see or hear anything?"

"No."

Pandora looked at me and cocked her head back toward Striker as if to tell me she approved. I glared at her in response. *Don't get used to him, he won't be around much ... I hope.*

"And just what were you doing at the library?"

I blew out a puff of air, disturbing a red curl that was dangling down across my forehead. Hadn't Augusta told him all this? "I was on my way to work, here, when I saw the lights on and the door open. I went in to investigate."

"Mew Mew," Pandora meowed. I wrinkled my brow at her—had her mew sounded like 'me, too'?

Striker continued as if he hadn't even heard the meow. "But you usually don't come to work that early, do you?"

I started to feel uneasy. Had he been asking around about me like he would ask around about a suspect? "I do usually try to get in earlier, but things don't always work out that way. That day I was a little late."

He narrowed his eyes. "I see. And what were you doing behind the library yesterday?"

"I told you yesterday. I was getting my cat." I pointed at Pandora who was now rubbing her face all over his ankles. To my surprise, he bent down to pet her.

Striker looked up at me from his crouched position. "Really? Are you sure that's all it was? Because I heard you like to get involved in cases and I don't need an amateur messing things up with this one."

Amateur?

"I was a pretty good crime journalist down south. In fact, there's more than one case that probably wouldn't have been solved without my help," I said indignantly, even as my traitorous cat purred loudly at his hands.

Striker stood up, causing Pandora to mewl with disappointment. "I know. I heard all about you. But I don't like anyone else looking into my cases. Besides, there's a killer on the loose and it could be dangerous. Best to leave this one to the pros."

And with that, he turned and walked out the door, robbing me of the chance to spear him with a nasty reply.

***

"Have you ever heard anyone be so rude and condescending?" I asked Pepper who was still staring at the door.

"He sure did grow up nice," she replied.

"What? He's a condescending jerk."

"Oh, I don't think you *really* think that."

I scrunched up my face. "What is wrong with you? Did you hear the way he talked to me?"

"I saw the way he *looked* at you ... and the way you looked at him," she said smugly. "I think there's a spark there. I could feel the heat myself—don't try to deny it."

The truth was I felt the heat, too, but at my age I just figured it was another hot flash.

"Pffttt..." I flapped my hand at her. I didn't like the way she was looking at me. Pepper loved playing matchmaker. "Now, don't go getting any ideas about fixing a special tea for me or Sheriff Meanie."

"I won't," she said innocently. Too innocently. I put my teacup down and made a mental note not to drink anything she served me any time in the near future.

"So anyway, what was this other thing you were starting to tell me before Eddie came in?" Pepper picked up her teacup and sipped.

I scrunched up my face. Sheriff Meanie had gotten me so worked up I'd forgotten what we'd been talking about.

"You told me about the fabric on the embosser and said there was something else..." Pepper prompted.

"Oh yes, the bronzes," I said, then told her what Josiah had told me about the old bronzes that had been donated to the library.

"Why would Ophelia be after bronze statues?" Pepper asked. "She already has enough money."

I shrugged. "Who knows? She seems money-hungry to me. Plus, with her background being married to an antique auctioneer, she'd know the value of them."

"But how would she even know they were there? Bates donated them long before she came to town and, as you said, everyone has pretty much forgotten about them. They aren't on display in there or anything, are they?"

"No. I remember noticing them once downstairs in the paperback section, but they aren't in the main section upstairs." Something niggled at the back of my mind. "Lavinia said that Ophelia had scoured the library, so she would have seen them."

"Did Lavinia say Ophelia was looking for the bronzes?"

"No, in fact she was kind of cagey about the whole thing." I picked up a molasses cookie and took a big bite, relishing the combination of sugar and spice. "But if we could match one of Ophelia's coats to that navy blue fabric, then we'd have something concrete."

Pepper wrinkled her nose. "I'm still not convinced Ophelia is the killer, but I do have a special tea for her. Maybe we could pay her a visit."

"You're not trying to make her nice with one of your teas are you?" I could only picture what would happen if that backfired like some of Pepper's other attempts. I shuddered to think of a meaner Ophelia Withington.

Pepper smiled. "Not trying to *make her nice*. Just restoring her faith and her natural personality."

I rolled my eyes.

"I know she always leaves the office at three p.m. and goes home to sort through her client list and match the new properties to potential clients," Pepper said. "We could stop by and catch her off-guard. I'll bring some tea and cookies and distract her and you can pretend you need to use the bathroom and look through her closet."

"That sounds perfect."

"So, I take it you're not going to heed Eddie's warning and step out of the investigation?"

"Heck, no." I gave Pepper my, 'you-know-me-better-than-that' look. "I'm going to do just what Lavinia asked and find her killer, even if it's the last thing I do."

Chapter Twelve

Ophelia Withington lived in a big, old barn converted into a house just outside of town. We stood on the granite slab doorstep—Pepper in her prim sweater set and plaid skirt and me in my plain old maroon turtleneck and faded jeans.

Pepper held a warming bag made from a bright paisley print at her side. She'd had the bags specially made so she could prepare tea at her shop and keep it warm for travel.

I wiped my sweaty palms on my jeans and rang the bell.

We heard some noises inside, and then the door opened to reveal a surprised-looking Ophelia Withington.

"Hi, Pepper." She started to half-smile until she saw me standing next to Pepper, then her face turned to an ugly frown. "Wilhelmina ... I hope you're not here to harass me again. If so, I'm calling the cops."

I held my hands up. "We come in peace."

She looked from me to Pepper skeptically, ready to slam the door in our faces.

Pepper held out the bag. "I made you some tea and cookies. I know the anniversary of Pete's passing is coming up and I thought it might help comfort you."

I shot a look at Pepper. She was really laying it on, but it seemed to work.

Ophelia's face softened. "Well, I *was* working ..."

"Oh, it will only be a few minutes." Pepper pushed her way inside. "I have the tea already hot right here in the bag."

"Err ... well, okay, but just for a short visit."

We both followed Pepper into the living room and watched her produce a tea towel, tray, teapot, creamer and bowl with tiny sugar cubes, cups, saucers and shortbread cookies from the bag.

"Shortbread cookies are my favorite." Ophelia looked at Pepper. "How did you know?"

"Oh, just a lucky guess." Pepper poured hot water from the tea kettle into a light blue cup, then took out a small tea bag and placed it inside. She repeated the process for two other cups, laid the cookies out on the tray, then sat back with her hands folded in her lap. "The tea needs to steep for a few minutes."

Ophelia looked as fidgety as I felt. Pepper produced some napkins stamped with her Tea Shoppe logo in gold and passed them out while we listened to the clock tick. Finally, when the silence was just about to become unbearable, Pepper picked up the blue cup and handed it to Ophelia.

"This should be perfect now." Pepper lifted a miniature silver creamer from the tray and lifted her brow to Ophelia, who nodded and pushed her cup toward Pepper so she could pour in the cream.

Pepper rummaged in the bag again and pulled out silver tongs, the ends in the shape of bird claws. She put the tongs in the sugar bowl and pushed it toward Ophelia who shook her head. Apparently, she didn't take sugar. I bit my tongue so I wouldn't urge her to take some, as it might make her less bitter.

Ophelia settled back in her seat, eyeing Pepper suspiciously. "So, what brings you by, really?"

"Well, truthfully, I know how down you've been since Pete died and I have a new line of herbal teas to soothe the soul. I thought it might help and, well, if it does, I know word of mouth is the best advertisement."

Ophelia screwed up her face. "I don't believe in that stuff."

"What? You mean herbs?" Pepper asked. "There are many medical studies about their effectiveness."

"Anyway, it's been a few years since Pete died." Ophelia sipped the tea and her voice softened. "I don't get nearly as upset as I used to."

I almost felt sorry for her until I saw Pepper looking at me pointedly and I remembered the real reason we'd come.

"I'd known Pete since I was a young girl," Pepper said. "My parents used to take me to his auctions. What are some of your fondest memories of him?"

Ophelia relaxed into her chair and smiled ... yes, she actually smiled. She opened her mouth to say something.

"Excuse me," I said as nicely as I could. "Could I use your bathroom?"

Ophelia barely looked in my direction as she waved a hand toward the hall. "Help yourself. It's down the hall on the left."

I got up, taking care not to knock over the tea tray in my excitement. I had to admit, whatever Pepper had put in that tea did seem to be mellowing Ophelia. As I started down the hall, I heard Ophelia telling Pepper about the day she and Pete met.

The hallway had three doors. One led to a study, one to the bathroom and the third to the hall closet. I opened the bathroom door and made a lot of noise shutting it, then crept over to the closet and opened it quietly.

I thumbed through the coats one at a time, my stomach sinking as I got closer to the end. Tan trench coat, black rain poncho, white wool jacket, a faux fur—or was it real? I had no idea how to tell. There were also several blazers and a tweed wool coat.

There was nothing in navy blue wool.

I eyed the stairway leading upstairs. A woman didn't keep all her coats in the hall closet, did she?

I could hear snatches of conversation from the living room. Ophelia was engrossed in her stories of Pete. She sounded almost pleasant. I felt a stab of guilt, but not enough to stop me from tiptoeing down the hall and creeping up the stairs.

Ophelia's bedroom was at the top of the stairs, and to the right was what looked like a spare bedroom. At my own house, I kept my overflow coats in the closet of the spare bedroom, so I turned right.

Trying to walk lightly so they wouldn't hear me downstairs, I slowly opened the closet door. I didn't have to look far...right in front of me was a big old wool cape ... in dark navy blue.

***

I had to stop myself from racing down the stairs—I didn't want Ophelia to hear me and know I'd been up there. I crept down them, keeping close to the sides so as to avoid any give-away squeaks. Then, once in the hall, I rushed down to the bathroom and flushed the toilet.

Back in the living room, Ophelia was still reminiscing about Pete, her back to me. Pepper looked over at me and I gestured wildly with a thumbs up, jerking my head toward the door to indicate we should get going.

Ophelia turned around and I quickly composed myself.

"Oh, Wilhelmina, I was just telling Pepper the funniest story—"

"That's great, Ophelia, but we really should be going." I looked at my wrist where a watch would have been if I wore one.

"Oh, so soon?" Ophelia looked crushed and I narrowed my eyes at Pepper. What the heck had she given her?

Pepper started to gather everything up and put it in the bag. "Yes, sorry. We do have to get back to our shops."

"Oh, of course." Ophelia stood and extended her hand to Pepper. "Thank you so much for stopping by. I feel much better now ... though I didn't even realize that I didn't feel good before."

"You're welcome. See, my teas really do work wonders." Pepper shook her hand then started toward the door.

"Oh, and Wilhelmina, I do hope you will excuse my nasty behavior at my office. It's just that ... well ... I wasn't in the library that morning and I guess I felt like you were accusing me."

"I was just checking on what I heard. I didn't mean to accuse you." Like heck I didn't, I thought, as I pictured the navy blue cape hanging in her closet.

I opened the door and pulled Pepper outside. Ophelia stood just inside the threshold, her hand on the door, about to close it.

"You know, there is one thing I remember from that morning that was strange." Ophelia said as we were walking away.

I turned back, wrinkling my brow at her. "What's that?"

"I *was* in town ... but not at the library." A pained look crossed her face and she shook her head. "Anyway, as I was leaving after doing my banking, a long black car went speeding past me up the mountain road. They were going very fast, driving recklessly, as if they wanted to get away from something fast. Nearly ran me off the road."

Chapter Thirteen

"See now, Ophelia isn't so bad, is she?" Pepper asked as she drove back to town in her yellow Fiat.

"Not so bad? I found a navy blue cape in her closet—she's probably the killer!"

Pepper glanced sideways at me. "Oh, come on. Didn't Myrna say she was wearing a raincoat?"

I pressed my lips together. "Yeah, but maybe Myrna was mistaken. I'm pretty sure that cape was the same color blue as the thread, and Lavinia said whoever pushed her was wearing a cape."

"Are you sure you aren't just so focused on the possibility that it could be Ophelia that you are blinded to anything else?" Pepper asked. "I mean, you saw how nice she was today."

"Yeah, what did you give her, anyway?"

"Oh just a special tea," Pepper said smugly.

"Well, nice or not she could be a killer." I pulled out my cell phone. "I should call Augusta and let her know Ophelia has a cape that matches the fibers on the murder weapon."

"Augusta ... or Eddie?" Pepper smirked.

"Very funny." I stared at my phone.

"What's wrong?" Pepper asked as she pulled into the municipal parking lot.

"I'm not really sure what to say. I can't very well tell Augusta I was in Ophelia's house rummaging through her closet and happened to discover a blue cape. And how would I explain that I know the killer wore a cape? Sheriff Meanie would probably arrest me if I came out with that."

Pepper parked the car, then reached in the back for her bag of tea items. "Sounds like you need something more solid ... something that will cause the police to search Ophelia's house and find the cape themselves."

"That's right. I need solid evidence." I opened my door and hopped out of the car. "I need to find a motive or place her at the scene of the crime."

Pepper fell in step beside me as I walked down the sidewalk toward our stores. The birds were chirping, the sun beaming down and buds starting to form on the trees, but I didn't notice any of it. I was too focused on figuring out what to do next.

"How are you going to do that?" Pepper asked.

"Her motive could have been the bronzes. Of course, they are valuable, but I wonder if Bates bought them from Pete? Maybe they have special meaning to her. I suppose I could talk to Bates about that."

I glanced sideways as we passed the library. Across the street, a side street opened up to the front of the church, the church that Ophelia had said she was lighting a candle at that morning. "I can't really do too much about her motive right now, but I can check out her alibi."

Pepper's eyes followed my gaze. "At the church?"

"Yep. She said she was lighting a candle. Maybe Pastor Foley saw her there and can verify the time and how long she stayed. Maybe he saw where she went afterward."

Pepper shrugged. "I guess it's worth a try. I think you're wasting your time, though, because I'm sure she didn't do it. Maybe you should be checking out that black car Ophelia said she saw instead."

"Maybe, but if I learned one thing as a crime journalist, it's that you've got to cover all your bases and check out *all* the leads thoroughly." I turned down the side street.

"You want some company?" Pepper called after me.

"No, thanks. This will only take a few minutes, then I'm going to grab Pandora from the shop and head home."

"Okay, see you tomorrow." Her words echoed down the street as I walked toward the church.

The First Hope church was one of the oldest buildings in Mystic Notch. I'd only been inside a handful of times. My family wasn't active in organized religion and I realized as I approached the large cathedral style doors that I didn't even know what kind of religion they practiced there.

Inside, the church was dimly lit. Rows of pews in dark oak lined the sides. The church was rather plain, painted in white. A large round stained glass window sat high in the gable end wall, casting shards of muted red and yellow light on the altar. Rows of large frosted glass rectangular windows with rounded tops lined the sides, but, surprisingly, didn't let in a lot of light. It was as quiet as a library and smelled like exotic spices.

I walked toward the front, the sound of my footsteps on the shiny marble floor echoing hollowly. Was Pastor Foley here somewhere?

As I approached the altar, a rustling sound to the left caught my attention and I noticed a hallway led out of the chapel to the side stairs. I followed it to a small room. Inside, a tiny gray-haired lady rummaged in a box exploding with wadded paper. She pulled something out and straightened.

I cleared my throat.

She whirled around, startled, keeping the item she'd taken from the box behind her back.

I recognized her as Emma Potts.

"Sorry. I hope I didn't startle you," I said. "I'm looking for Pastor Foley."

"He's not here. I'm the church secretary, though. Can I help you?" She peered at me through the thick lenses of her eyeglasses. "I don't believe I know you ... are you a church member?"

I took a step into the room. "It's me, Wilhelmina Chance."

Her brows dipped in a V as she studied me. "Oh, that's right. Anna's granddaughter who went down south quite a few years ago."

"That's right. I inherited my grandmother's bookstore, so I'm back to stay now."

Emma pushed her glasses up on her nose with her free hand, keeping the hand with the object she'd retrieved from the box behind her back. "What can I do for you? Any relative of Anna's is a friend of mine."

"Well, I'm sure you heard about Lavinia Babbage..."

"Yes, that's so sad. She was part of our flock, you know. Dedicated to helping others and always donated to our causes ... which we are in dire need of money for." Her face crumbled with sadness and she shook her head. I heard a jingling noise come from behind her. What the heck did she have back there and why was she hiding it?

I leaned to the left trying to see what was behind her and she leaned in the same direction to block me.

"So, what can I help you with?" she prompted.

I straightened back up. "Well, it's just that I found her and I'd like to follow up on a few things.

I feel a bit responsible for helping to bring her killer to justice."

"Oh, well, that seems reasonable, but how can *I* help with that?"

"I was looking into who was in town that morning and someone saw Ophelia Withington here at the church."

Emma's back stiffened at the mention of Ophelia's name, and her face took on a sour look.

I continued, "She said she was here and I was wondering if you saw her."

"Here? At the church? Certainly not. Why, she's done everything she can to..." Emma let her voice trail off and looked around as if to make sure no one had heard her.

"To what?" I prompted.

"Well, let's just say she was no friend of the church," Emma said primly. "Just what did she say she was doing here?"

"She said she was lighting a candle for Pete."

Emma huffed. "Well, that right there proves she was lying."

"Why's that?"

"This church doesn't have candles."

Chapter Fourteen

Pandora was waiting for me in the bookshop window. I unlocked the door, cashed out the register and then locked up again. We trotted to the Jeep together.

I glanced back toward the church as I drove out of the parking lot.

"So, Ophelia lied about lighting a candle at the church ... which makes me wonder what else she lied about," I said out loud.

"Meow." Pandora blinked at me, her luminescent eyes taking on more of a green tint in the afternoon light.

"But, then again, that also means that Lavinia lied about lighting a candle."

Pandora licked her front paw, running it behind her ear a few times.

"Why would they both lie? Did the two of them share a secret? And, if so, did that have anything to do with Lavinia's death?"

"Meoow!" A gray paw snaked out and tapped my arm.

"What?" I looked at Pandora who simply withdrew her paw, but not before snagging her claw on the fabric of my turtleneck.

"Ahh, geez." I twisted my arm, looking at the pinprick-sized hole in my shirt. "Thanks a lot."

"Mew." She curled into a ball and purred noisily all the way home.

I pulled into the driveway, and instead of racing me to the back door, Pandora trotted off toward the path that led to Elspeth's house.

"Hey, where are you going? Don't you want supper?" I yelled after her.

She responded by flicking her tail at me and breaking into a run.

"Sheesh, I must be lonelier than I thought. Now I'm talking to the cat," I said out loud to no one. Thoughts of Sheriff Striker invaded my head. He *was* kind of cute, but I wasn't really sure I wanted to get involved with anyone right now. My marriage had ended badly only a few years ago and the thought of going through anything like that again didn't appeal to me.

Of course, no one said I had to marry the guy, I thought as I looked at the empty cat bowl. It sure did feel like the house was missing something without Pandora. My eye went to the pie plate and carrier I'd washed that morning. Might as well follow in Pandora's paw steps and return it to Elspeth.

I shrugged on a sweater and boots, then headed out through the woods carrying the pie plate and carrier inside the bag Elspeth had sent them over in. It was less than a ten-minute walk to Elspeth's and I could see her sitting on her porch as I approached the house. She was wrapped in a green crocheted shawl, her right arm held straight out and resting on the porch railing, a pile of birdseed in her open palm.

I watched in wonder as a gray tufted titmouse landed on her hand and pecked at the seeds. A brown chickadee bobbed his head up and down on the rose vine, twittering loudly as he waited for his turn at the buffet of seeds and nuts Elspeth offered.

The birds flew off as I approached the porch. "Sorry, didn't mean to scare away your friends."

"Oh, that's okay. I've been feeding them by hand for years now. They'll be back tomorrow." Elspeth stood and leaned over the railing, wiping her hands together and letting the seeds fall into the garden.

"I brought your pie plate back. The pie was delicious." I set the bag down on the porch as Elspeth settled back into her wicker chair.

"Meow." Pandora peeked out from behind Elspeth and I noticed the orange tiger cat sitting next to her. A Siamese lay at the foot of Elspeth's chair, and a big jet-black tomcat sat off to the side.

"I figured you had run over here," I said to Pandora who came over and rubbed herself against my ankles.

"Have a seat." Elspeth gestured to a green wooden rocking chair. I sat and Pandora jumped into my lap.

"I was wondering what you know of Ophelia Withington." Pandora dug her claws into my leg and the orange cat hissed.

"Shush, Tigger," Elspeth said to the cat. "Ophelia isn't a bad person ... she just got a little lost when Pete died."

"Someone saw her around the library at the time Lavinia was killed." I looked at Elspeth. "Do you think she could have done it? Did Ophelia and Lavinia have some sort of grudge or secret?"

"Secret?" Why do you ask that?"

I chose my words carefully. I couldn't tell Elspeth that Lavinia's ghost had lied to me about lighting a candle. "Oh ... just something I found out when I was asking around."

"So, you *are* looking into Lavinia's murder?" Elspeth nodded. "I figured you would."

I didn't have a good comeback for that so I just shrugged.

"I don't think anyone killed Lavinia on purpose, especially not Ophelia. She does have her demons, but she's no killer." Elspeth glanced out into the woods and her eyes took on a faraway look. "Do you remember living in Mystic Notch as a little girl?"

I felt my lips curl in a smile. I had happy childhood memories. "Yes."

"Didn't it seem like a magical place?"

"Of course. I loved pretending there were magic fairies in the woods and time spent with my grandmother was always special. Those were happy times." I remembered that time spent with my grandmother always involved lots of reading. We shared a love of books, which was probably why she'd left me the bookstore.

As a child, I'd read voraciously. Maybe I'd been a bit too much of a bookworm. I'd gotten so involved in some of the books I'd read that I could almost remember some of them coming true. It was probably just my memory fooling with me, but I swore that some of the objects from the books I'd read had appeared in my room.

Like that worn stuffed rabbit I'd had as a child and that favorite locket I had later on as a teen. It seemed like those had been identical to the ones in books I'd read, but I'd probably bought them in the store because they reminded me of the book—my selective memory just didn't remember actually buying them.

"I bet you never felt that way down south." Elspeth's words pulled me away from my thoughts.

I shrugged, wondering what this had to do with Lavinia's death. "Once you grow up, you lose that carefree, magical feeling you have when you're a kid."

"But, maybe you felt some of that magic when you came back here ... or shortly before you made your decision to come back."

My breath caught in my throat. Was Elspeth referring to my strange ability to see ghosts? Certainly, some might think that was magical although I thought it was just a pain in the butt. No, she was probably just referring to that 'coming home' feeling that I did experience when I finally made the decision to move back.

As if reading my thoughts, Elspeth said, "Well, it always feels like magic coming home. But Mystic Notch is special. Don't you feel it?"

She stuck out her hand, waving it back and forth. To my astonishment, a bright yellow and black butterfly drifted over, landed on her pinkie finger and flexed its wings back and forth in the air. Wasn't it too early in the season for butterflies?

I nodded and stroked Pandora's silky fur, mesmerized by the slow flexing of the butterfly's wings.

"Magic can be good," Elspeth said, turning her keen blue eyes on me. "But just remember, it isn't *always* good. There's always been an age-old battle between good and evil. One must be careful not to let evil get the upper hand."

She lifted her hand high in the air and the butterfly flew away. My head felt a little foggy and I took a deep breath. That was some strange stuff she was talking about.

My heart pinched with concern ... I hoped Elspeth wasn't getting dementia. She was quite old. I wrinkled my brow in thought—just how old was she? I realized I had no idea. She'd always been my grandmother's neighbor, since I was little. She seemed old even then, but that was from the perspective of a child.

The wind chimes tinkled softly in the corner of the porch and I glanced over at them, watching their bronze tubes rub together in the breeze. Elspeth would remember the bronzes being donated to the library, so maybe she would know who might want to steal them?

"Do you remember anything about Idris Bates giving bronzes to the library back in the sixties?" I asked.

Elspeth shivered and I realized it was getting colder out. "I don't remember anything about bronzes, but Idris Bates is one you should steer clear of."

Elspeth pulled her shawl tighter and stood up. "I'm getting a bit chilled. Would you like to go inside?"

"No, I'd better get home and rustle up some dinner. I just wanted to return your pie plate and carrier." I stood, dumping Pandora from my lap. She landed on the porch floor with a soft thud, then let out a muted "mew", shook herself and trotted over to the stairs.

Elspeth opened the door while I started down the steps after Pandora.

I turned around, walking backwards for a few steps. "Thanks for the pie, it was delicious."

"You're welcome. Be careful on the way home."

I turned around, waving to her over my shoulder, and followed Pandora into the woods.

"What was she talking about, Pandora?" I asked, glancing backwards over my shoulder at Elspeth's house. "All that magic talk didn't make much sense."

Pandora glanced up at me but kept trotting along beside me.

"Was she trying to warn me?"

"Meow!"

"Don't tell me magic has anything to do with Lavinia's murder ... I don't believe in that stuff."

"Oh, you don't?" Lavinia's ghost appeared beside me and I practically fainted. You'd think I'd be getting used to ghosts appearing out of nowhere by now, but it still startled me.

"Jeepers. Will you stop doing that?" I pleaded.

"What? Appearing? That's what ghosts do," Lavinia said, gliding along beside me. "Anyway, you were just telling your cat you don't believe in magic."

I frowned at Pandora. Had I become one of those crazy cat ladies who talk to their cats?

"Of course I don't believe in magic."

"Then I suppose you don't believe in ghosts, either."

I chewed on my bottom lip. Two years ago, I probably would have said I didn't believe in ghosts, but now with Lavinia's ghost gliding along happily beside me I could hardly say that anymore. Maybe just because I hadn't experienced magic didn't mean that it didn't exist. Maybe I should give more consideration to what Elspeth had said.

Did magic have something to do with Lavinia's murder?

As if reading my mind, Lavinia said, "So, are you making progress finding my murderer? I heard you telling Pepper about the embosser you found behind the library."

I glanced over at her. "You were eavesdropping?"

"Not really. I was just floating around in the back of the store and heard you."

I had no idea the ghosts floated around when I couldn't see them and it kind of creeped me out. "Then you heard about the navy blue fabric?"

"Yeeees."

"I found a navy blue cape in Ophelia Withington's closet."

Lavinia gasped. "You don't say? A cape? I remember it seemed like the killer was wearing a cape, but I only saw a shadow. So, why didn't you tell the police and have her arrested?"

Pandora let out a yowl beside me and Lavinia reached down to pet her, all the while gliding along perfectly beside me without even slowing down.

"Well, that's the problem. I can't really tell them I know about the cape, because I'm pretty sure they won't believe I talk to ghosts, and if I tell them I just went through her closet they might get mad. I need more proof." I thought about my visit to the church and how they didn't have any candles. Lavinia had said she'd been in town early to light a candle ... that's how she saw someone in the library in the first place.

"Lavinia, you said you were at the church lighting a candle that morning, but I stopped by today and there's no ca—"

"Ooops, gotta go." Lavinia cut me off and then promptly vanished.

I stared at the empty space where Lavinia's ghost was just seconds ago. Pandora looked up at me, and I swear she shrugged. Something fishy was going on at the church—why was Lavinia acting so secretive about it? Did it have something to do with her death?

My house came into view and I noticed clouds had rolled in, turning the sky as ominous as my thoughts. There were too many unanswered questions.

Why had Lavinia *and* Ophelia lied about the church? Had Lavinia really been murdered because she just happened across someone stealing the bronzes? And what was all this magic talk Elspeth was spouting?

I didn't know the answers to any of these questions, so I turned my thoughts to the one thing I could do—figure out a way to tip Augusta off to the navy blue cape hanging in Ophelia's closet.

Chapter Fifteen

The next morning, I wasn't any closer to figuring out how to tip Augusta off about the blue cape. Maybe the best course was to tell her I'd seen the fiber on the embosser and then let her know that Ophelia had a blue cape. I didn't have to mention that Lavinia had told me about a cape or that I'd searched Ophelia's closets. I could just pretend I'd seen Ophelia wearing it.

Of course, it would be better if I knew Ophelia's motive. I made a mental note to check in the library for the bronzes. If one was missing, then all I would need to do would be to find out who had it and I'd have the killer. Hopefully, I would see it in Ophelia's house. I didn't recall seeing one on my visit, but I guess if I killed a librarian and stole a valuable bronze, I'd hide it somewhere, too.

But first, I had to head out to Barry's and pick up those books. Lavinia's funeral was in the afternoon and I planned to catalogue some of the books at the store before that, so I threw on my jeans and a pink sweater, then tossed my black wrinkle-free polyester dress, black sheer nylons and pumps into a bag to change into later.

I usually didn't bother too much with my hair, but I tried to force the curls into waves that framed my face instead of the unruly red mop it usually arranged itself into. It was, after all, Lavinia's funeral and I wanted to look halfway decent.

Pandora and I did our usual morning routine of cat food and corn flakes, then got into the Jeep and headed out to Barry's.

The air was crisp, the light blue sky dotted with clouds. The heavy clouds had rolled out after the overnight rain, but at the edge of the horizon it looked like a new storm was coming. As I drove the mountain roads, I noticed the birds and squirrels actively foraging in the woods for nuts and seeds as they usually did before a storm. I kept watch on the sides of the roads for moose or deer. They often crossed the road at this time of morning and an accident with one of them could be fatal for either one of us, so it paid to keep one's eyes open.

There weren't many other cars out this early. I passed Myrna on her way into town, then turned on the road that led higher up into the mountains toward Barry's. The road was narrow and I noticed a familiar black pick-up truck coming down the other way.

Whose car was that? I squinted toward it and recognized the head of white hair. Bing Thorndike.

I raised my hand in a greeting, but he didn't seem to see me, his eyes focused on the road, which he was traveling down rather fast.

"I wonder where he's going?"

Pandora sneezed and hopped into the back, running to the hatch to stand up and look out the back window.

A few seconds later, I pulled down the lonely road that led to Barry's, then drove my Jeep up the gravel driveway and parked in front of his 1800s farm house. Next to the house was a big barn he used as his antique shop. The shop wasn't open yet, so he'd told me to come right to the house where he was holding the box of books for me.

I cut the engine, then turned to Pandora, who had hopped back into the passenger seat. "You stay here."

She narrowed her eyes at me. Then, as I opened my door, she shot out and ran onto Barry's front porch.

I slipped out of the Jeep, wincing in surprise as I landed on my bad leg. The pain had been getting much better and I'd almost even forgotten about it, but I must have twisted it or something, because it was throbbing now.

I rested for a few seconds, stretching my leg and wishing I had some *Iced Fire* to rub on it, then started toward the porch. A cloud passed over the sun, sending a chill into the air, as I stepped onto the old wooden boards. A light wind kicked up some of fall's leftover leaves and I watched them swirl around the steps in a circle.

Barry had put his screen door on already—or still had it on from last summer—I wasn't sure which. I wrapped my hand around the iron handle, thick with layers of green paint, and pulled it open with a squeak. Raising my fist, I tapped on the wooden door, my heart leaping in my throat when it swung open under the light pressure of my tap.

"Barry?" I peeked through the crack of the open door, not sure if he meant for me to just walk in.

He didn't answer, and I felt the roots of doubt spreading in my stomach.

"Hello. It's me, Willa," I said even louder.

"Mew!" Pandora looked up at me impatiently then pushed her way through the door, causing it to swing open. She trotted into the living room, sniffed the air, then headed toward the kitchen.

I stepped inside, my heartbeat drumming in my veins, uncertain of what I would find. The old, wide pine floorboards creaked eerily as I made my way through the living room.

"Barry, I'm here!" I tried one more time.

"Meeoww!" Pandora's howl quickened my pace and I rounded the corner to the kitchen at breakneck speed, my heart leaping in my chest as I skidded to a stop, right before stepping on Barry's body.

"Barry!" I squealed. He didn't move, and my first thought was how suspicious Striker was going to be when he discovered I'd found another body.

Then Barry groaned, which scared the crap out of me. Then I realized he wasn't dead and relief flooded through me. I knelt down beside him on the yellow linoleum floor.

"Barry, what happened? Are you okay?"

"Wha?" Barry tried to push himself up then fell back. He rose up on his elbows and shook his head, looking at me with unfocused eyes.

I took his hand. "I'm going to call nine-one-one."

"No, wait a sec." His voice was thick, but his eyes seemed to be focusing better. He sat up and rubbed his face with his hands. "What happened?"

Pandora sniffed his pant legs, then rubbed her face against his hip. He scratched her behind the ears.

"I have no idea. I came over to get those books and found you here on the floor." I looked around the old country kitchen. There was a box on the floor with various silver items in it. A silver candlestick, pie server and pitcher sat on the table next to a laptop. Nothing seemed out of place and it didn't look like there had been a struggle. "Did you pass out?"

He tilted his head, his eyes narrowed to slits. "You know, I'm not sure. I guess I must have."

He struggled to his feet and I helped him into a chair, then sat at the old pine trestle table across from him. Pandora took the opportunity to sniff around the room.

"Have you ever passed out like that before?" I asked.

He shook his head. "Never."

"Does your head hurt? Did you hit it on something?" *Or did someone hit him*, I wondered.

Barry touched the back of his head, then the sides. "Nope, doesn't hurt at all."

"We should call nine-one-one and have you checked out."

"No. I feel fine now. I'd rather call my doctor and make an appointment."

I narrowed my eyes at him. Folks up here could be stubborn and I hoped he wasn't just putting me off. "Well, if you promise you'll call ..."

"I will." He looked around the kitchen. "It's funny—I don't remember passing out, though."

"What *do* you remember?"

"I was in here, cataloguing the silver I bought at Dodd's auction." Barry gestured to the items in front of them on the table, then a shadow crossed his face. "Wait a minute. Someone came to the door ..."

The hairs on the back of my neck started to tingle and my leg throbbed. I remembered how easily the door had swung open when I arrived. It wasn't unusual for people to leave their doors unlocked in Mystic Notch, but Barry's door hadn't even been shut all the way—almost as if someone had left in a hurry and only loosely closed the door behind them.

"Who came to the door?"

"I'm not sure." Barry's forehead creased in concentration. "One of the Bates brothers, I think. No, everything is so fuzzy, I might be imagining that."

I remembered the way Bing was driving down the road, as if he was in a hurry. "Was it Bing Thorndike?"

"I don't think so. Now that I'm thinking about it, I'm not really sure anyone was here at all. I saw Carson Bates at the auction last night and my memory is getting confused."

"What was Carson doing at an auction? Surely they already have enough antiques at home." My mind drifted to the bronzes in the library. The Bates family had so many antiques they could afford to donate them.

"Apparently, Felicity sold off some stuff at a yard sale and he was looking to get some of it back.

Old family heirlooms and such. He was going on about some books, quite insistent. Wanted to know if I'd come across them."

"Oh, right. I remember Derek came by the shop wanting to know if I had some old family scrapbooks."

Barry laughed. "I guess Felicity needs to find clever ways to get at the Bates money. She always was kind of strange. Come to think of it Carson's kind of strange, too."

I nodded in agreement, looking around the room. "You're not missing anything?"

Barry glanced around, looked at the silver on the table and in the box. "Nope, everything is here. Now that I think about it, I'm sure no one came ... my memory's just a little screwed up. Anyway, I have that box of books for you over here." Barry retrieved a cardboard banana box from the pantry.

I noticed he was steady on his feet and my worry for him started to subside as I peeked into the box, eager to check out the books. An old leather-bound was on the top and my stomach flitted with excitement as I pulled it out.

Barry frowned at the book, then looked into the box. "That's strange. I'm sure I put the leatherbound on the bottom. I wanted to surprise you with the best book last."

"Oh?" I frowned, only half-hearing him, my attention riveted on the beautifully preserved book. My fingers caressed the soft leather as I carefully opened the front to look at the publishing information. The musty smell of old paper hit my nose and I closed my eyes to breathe it in. I loved that smell.

Barry pressed his lips together as he thumbed through the books. "Maybe I don't remember, though. I might have switched them around. I'm not remembering correctly because of passing out."

I set the book aside and looked into the box, pulling out some of the books and stacking them on the table.

"Is there anything good in there?" Barry asked.

I tapped the leather-bound. "This one is pretty good. It's not a first edition, but I could probably get a couple hundred for it."

"Good. I want to repay you for those silver nut dishes, so I hope there's something else good in there."

I picked some more books out of the box. "There are some great children's books here and a few classics that are always popular. I'll have to do some research to see if there are any rare editions, but I'd say I'll make a pretty penny. What do I owe you?"

Barry waved his hand in the air. "Forget about it. I only paid a couple of bucks at a yard sale."

"You sure? I took the buck from you for the silver dishes."

Barry laughed. "You can buy me a coffee next time we see each other at an auction."

"Deal." I pushed up from the table and grabbed the box, hefting it onto my hip. "I hope you're really feeling okay."

"Don't worry, I'm feeling fine." Barry wrestled the box away from me. "Let me take this to your car for you."

I followed Barry to the front door. Pandora was fervently sniffing the threshold and she looked up at me. "Meow."

"Yes, we're going now," I said.

I could have sworn she made a face. "Meeeooow."

"What is with your cat?" Barry asked.

"I have no idea. She's probably cranky because she misses her soft cat bed." We crossed the threshold and Pandora gave me what seemed like an exasperated look before following us to the Jeep.

I took the box and loaded it in the back. Pandora hopped up on the tailgate and made her way to the passenger seat. "Well, thanks for picking these up. If you see any more, feel free to grab them. I'm woefully low on stock."

"Will do. You do the same for me. Anything silver at a reasonable price."

"Okay." I hopped into the Jeep and started it up while Barry made his way back into the house.

I drove toward town, feeling uneasy. Finding Barry lying on the floor had unnerved me. Pandora put a comforting paw on my thigh and I felt my heart surge. Could it be I was really getting attached to the fur ball?

"Doesn't it seem odd that a healthy young guy like Barry would pass out for no reason?" I said out loud, then realized no one was in the car except me and Pandora.

"Mew." Pandora nodded her head.

"But, if someone was there, surely Barry would remember. And if they hit him to knock him out, surely he'd feel the lump on his head, wouldn't he?"

I snuck a look at Pandora, but she merely gave me a blank stare

"And why would someone knock him out? It didn't seem like anything was taken. All his silver was there and the books were all in the box, although he did think the leather book had been moved."

"Mew."

"But, who would do that?" My mind drifted back to the truck I'd seen racing down the hill. Bing's truck.

"Probably just coincidence, right?" I turned to Pandora.

"Meow."

"I guess it's a mystery," I said to Pandora. "Probably has nothing to do with Lavinia's murder, though, and that's what I need to focus on today."

Pandora let out a string of meow's and, for a second, I thought it sounded like "*you never know.*"

I shut my mouth and focused on the road. Not only was I getting into the bad habit of talking to my cat, but now I thought she was actually answering me. I really did need to get a social life.

Chapter Sixteen

I parked in the small parking lot behind my store since I had the box of books to lug inside. I went in through the back and dropped off the books. When I finally got to the front, I could see Cordelia, Hattie and Josiah waiting outside with coffee mugs in their hands. I rushed to open the door for them.

"I was wondering if you were going to make it today." Josiah handed me a Styrofoam cup and I practically swooned with gratitude. The happenings out at Barry's had made me late for my morning caffeine fix.

"Sorry," I said in-between sips. "I had to pick up a box of books this morning and it took me longer than I expected."

"Oh, that's no problem," Cordelia twittered. I noticed she and Hattie were dressed in matching polyester pantsuits—Hattie's in lemon yellow and Cordelia's in lime green. They wore the same exact lemon and lime colored blouses underneath the jackets.

"Well, don't you ladies look nice," I said.

"Thanks," Cordelia answered for both of them. "Lavinia's funeral is today, you know."

"Yes, I'm going," I said, my attention captured by a light, misty swirl coming from the end of the biography row. Was it Lavinia listening in again?

"I imagine most of the town will turn out," Josiah said. "Everyone knew her from the library."

"Where's Bing?" I asked, suddenly realizing he was missing.

"Oh, he called this morning," Josiah answered. "Said he didn't feel good this morning and not to worry about him if he didn't show up."

I frowned at my coffee. He sure looked okay when I saw him rushing down the road. Then again, maybe he was rushing to the doctor's office.

"Did you find out any more about those bronzes?" Hattie asked.

"No. You?"

She shook her head. "Some of the old-timers remember them being donated, but no one knew they were valuable."

I caught a glimpse of Pandora trotting over to the biography row and watched her swat at the mist out of the corner of my eye.

"I was going to close up early today and check them out at the library before I headed out to Lavinia's funeral," I said.

"Good idea." Hattie nodded. "I'm sure the police must be looking at them by now."

"We don't even know if the police know about them." Cordelia turned to me. "Did you mention them to Augusta?"

I shook my head.

"Not yet." I'd been too busy snooping around in Ophelia's house.

"Well, you probably have work to do seeing as it's a short day, and I have to get home and start getting spiffed up for the funeral." Josiah started toward the door.

"Come on, sister. We need to get some tea over at Pepper's and then take a little nap before we go to Lavinia's service." Cordelia grabbed Hattie's elbow and they followed Josiah to the door.

Josiah opened it and gestured for the ladies to precede him. They stepped through, then turned back to me. "See you there, Willa."

I nodded and waved, then the three of them spilled out onto the street and the door shut, leaving me alone in the store. Well, alone as far as earthly inhabitants go, that is.

The swirling mist at the end of the biography row glided toward me, slowly forming into the shape of Lavinia. "So, you're going to my funeral?"

"Of course. The killer might be there. Maybe I can pick her out."

"Her?"

"My money is on Ophelia, although I have to admit I still can't figure out her motive."

"Oh yes, you found that blue cape. I remember that cape, now that you mention it. She used to wear that out a lot with Pete." Lavinia leaned in toward me. "Haven't seen her wear it since he died."

"So? You're not trying to tell me she wouldn't have been wearing it, are you?"

Lavinia shrugged. "I just think you might have blinders on here. Maybe you should consider some other suspects."

"I don't *have* any other suspects."

"Because you haven't been looking. It's never good to focus on one thing. Besides, my feeling is there may be more to this than meets the eye."

"What do you mean by that?"

"Maybe there are other forces at work."

"Other forces?" I scrunched up my face at her. Now she was starting to sound like Elspeth.

"Oh bother," Lavinia waved her hand in the air, making a swirly trail of misty goo that hung suspended for a few seconds before falling to the ground and evaporating. "What other clues do you have?"

"Well, Ophelia did say she saw a long, dark car speeding away from town that morning." My leg was starting to throb, so I turned back toward the front of the store where I kept a tube of *Iced Fire*. Lavinia floated along beside me, Pandora at her heels.

"See? Now, that's a clue you should be looking into." Lavinia suggested. "And what about the bronzes?"

"You know about those?"

"I overheard you talking about them yesterday. I had forgotten all about them until you mentioned them. They're downstairs, just like you said."

"How many are there?"

"Four. At first we had them on display upstairs, but then people's tastes changed and Western stuff wasn't as popular. We moved them downstairs decades ago," Lavinia said. "Do you think I stumbled across someone trying to steal them and they did me in?"

"Maybe." I plopped onto the sofa, then pulled up leg of my jeans and rubbed some *Iced Fire* on my leg. Pandora came over to investigate, sniffed at my leg, yowled and ran to the back of the store.

Lavinia laughed. "That *is* a rather potent smell."

"Yeah, but it works wonders."

Two misty figures materialized before us— Franklin Pierce and Robert Frost—and they were both holding their noses.

"Iced fire? Will the world end in fire or ice? I know not, but either way I hope it doesn't smell like *that*," Frost said, pointing down at the tube.

Pierce and Lavinia burst out laughing at the poetry reference. I didn't think it was so funny. Did I really smell that bad?

"I heard you talking about bronzes, and I do say some are quite valuable." Franklin Pierce looked at us importantly. "In fact, I could boast that there were a few bronze busts made of me in my day."

"That's right," Lavinia said. "We have one in the library."

"I've had one or two made of me as well," Frost said, not to be outdone. "In fact, mine was so valuable it was stolen from its spot at Wichita State University some years back."

Pierce narrowed his ghostly eyes at Frost. "I heard that was a drunken prank."

Frost shrugged. "Whatever. Anyway, I dare say the scoundrel that killed Lavinia might have been after those bronzes. Money makes people do strange things."

Pierce nodded. "On that, I concur."

"Your theory on the bronzes could be a good one," Lavinia said. "But I don't think Ophelia would be breaking into the library to steal them. It's just not her style."

I had to admit, Lavinia was right about that. But I *wanted* to continue thinking it was Ophelia. Mostly because I didn't like her and if the killer turned out to be her then I wouldn't feel bad. Plus

I had some good clues pointing to her and I knew there was a secret between her and Lavinia ... that secret might be the true motive.

On the other hand, maybe I *had* been ignoring other clues because I'd been so focused on Ophelia. Bing had been acting strangely ... did his odd behavior have anything to do with Lavinia's death? I certainly hoped not. Bing had been almost like a grandfather to me for as long as I could remember. I'd much rather the killer ended up being Ophelia.

And what about the weird thing with Barry this morning? It had looked like Bing was driving away from his house. Barry thought someone had been looking in the box of books ... but what would books have to do with anything?

I looked up and realized all three ghosts were staring at me expectantly.

"I plan to go to the library and see if the bronzes are there before I go to your funeral," I said to Lavinia.

"That sounds like a good idea," she replied. "But don't be so focused on one path that you are blind to the others."

"That's right." Robert winked at me. "Sometimes it's best to take the path less traveled."

"Well, I think we should be off." Lavinia linked her arms through the two men's elbows. "Shall we?"

They both nodded and the three of them disappeared, leaving me sitting on the sofa, blinking at nothing.

"Wait." The word tripped off my lips and fell into the silent room. I had wanted to ask Lavinia about the candles in the church, but she'd disappeared too fast.

I waved my hands at the empty space in frustration. I had been so sure the killer was Ophelia, but Lavinia had sprinkled my thoughts with doubt, and now I had to take some of the other clues more seriously.

That didn't mean I was going to drop Ophelia off the suspect list, though. I was still going to tell Augusta about that blue cape just as soon as I could. In the meantime, I'd just have to broaden my investigation to include some of the other clues ... even if it meant investigating an old friend.

Chapter Seventeen

More clouds had rolled in while I was in the bookstore and the somber atmosphere in the library echoed the weather outside. Lavinia's assistant, Myrtle, who, I supposed, was the new head librarian, sat mournful and lonely behind the big rounded desk.

I found myself thinking that if Myrtle *did* get the head librarian position, then she had benefitted from Lavinia's death. Standing in the doorway, I studied the short, bespectacled octogenarian. She must have weighed all of eighty pounds and I doubted she had enough strength to push Lavinia, never mind smash her on the head with the embosser. She was too short. And anyway, who would kill someone over a librarian job?

I walked into the library, nodding at Myrtle as I passed by. I'd changed into my wrinkle-free black dress and it swirled just above my knees while my heels made clickity-clack noises on the marble floor as I walked toward the back. I noticed the flag was at half-mast and Pierce's bust was draped with a black band. Apparently, they were taking Lavinia's death hard here.

I turned the corner to the back steps and a chill ran up my spine as I remembered finding Lavinia crumpled at the bottom of them. I hesitated a second, picturing the scene.

"Go on down," a voice whispered, startling me and almost sent me falling down the stairs. It was Lavinia swirling beside me. Why hadn't I just sent her over to look for the bronzes and saved myself a trip? She nodded pointedly at the stairs and started down.

Stepping gingerly down the stone stairs, I turned right at the landing and walked into the main library area, my footsteps growing silent as the hard stone floor changed to carpeting.

The bottom floor of the library was like a maze. Tightly packed rows of ten-foot high bookshelves were laid out with barely three feet of aisle space between them. There were various sections and rooms off the main room that one could wander into. It seemed always to be void of other humans and entombed in silence—the massive amount of books and carpeted flooring absorbed most of the noise. I'd gotten lost down there more than once.

"Where are they?" I whispered to Lavinia. My question was met with silence.

I looked beside me, then turned to look behind me, scanning for any sign of a ghost. Nothing ... not a faint swirl of mist ... not even a drop of condensation. Figures she'd disappear when I needed her most.

I decided to do the search methodically, row by row. The most likely place to display the bronzes was at the end of the rows or in one of the many alcoves, so moving along the perimeter would be my best choice.

I turned left, then walked to the end of the row where I was met with another row of books.

"Okay, maybe the bronzes are at the other end," I said softly, just in case Lavinia was listening and might offer her help.

I started down the row, then noticed a little alcove off to the left. "Is it here?" I whispered.

I took the sharp corner and almost jumped out of my shiny black pumps. Standing in front of me was Sheriff Eddie Striker ... and he didn't look happy.

***

"Were you talking to someone?" Striker's gray eyes drilled into mine, then shifted to look behind me.

"Me? No." He was standing in front of a two-foot square alcove indented in the wall. I tried to peer around his wide chest to see what was in the alcove and caught sight of a mahogany pedestal ... was a bronze on top of it?

"What are you doing here?" he asked.

"What are *you*?" My hands fisted on my hips and my brows dipped in an angry V. I felt like we'd been through this routine before. At least he wasn't pointing a gun at me this time.

His lips curled in that annoying half-smile and butterflies flittered in my stomach. I suddenly felt glad I'd made an attempt to tame my hair, and then immediately admonished myself for feeling that way. What did I care about looking good?

"Don't tell me you were coming here to borrow a book dressed like that." His gaze wandered from my face, down my body to my shoes and back up, lingering in some places longer than others.

I crossed my arms over my chest, feeling self-conscious about my clingy dress and scarred leg. At least the leg wasn't one of the parts where his gaze had lingered. It started to ache as if it knew I was thinking about it and I shifted my weight onto my right leg.

"What's wrong with what I'm wearing?"

"Nothing," he shrugged. "But I don't think you got all dressed up to borrow a book. You're up to something and my detective skills tell me you're here for the same reason I am."

"Oh? And what's that?"

Striker stepped aside to reveal what was on top of the pedestal ... a bronze statue of a cowboy on a bucking bronco in amazing detail. It was a deep

142

chocolate color and I knew if I touched it, it would feel silky, but hard and cold. Which was exactly the same way Striker was looking at me right now.

"There are four of them," I blurted out.

"I know. They're all here."

"Are they really that valuable?" I asked.

"I just had an expert here and he said only one is original, but even the recasts are worth thousands." Striker glanced back at the bronze. "The library is moving them out today and putting them somewhere more secure."

"How did you find out about them?"

"Probably the same way you did. I'm investigating the case and got a lead. But see, there's a difference between me investigating and you investigating." He paused and fixed me with a serious look. "I'm a cop and you're not. So *you* shouldn't be following up on leads."

"I'm just curious by nature," I said weakly. "So you think someone was trying to steal the bronzes and Lavinia stumbled onto them?"

Striker shrugged. "That's one possible motive. But seeing as the bronzes are still here, it's not likely."

I frowned at the statue. "Why not?"

"Don't you think the thief would have grabbed at least one of them after going to all the trouble of clobbering Lavinia?"

"But what if he got scared off? Maybe he didn't have time." Maybe I had scared him off when I came into the library. An icy chill ran up my spine when I realized I might have suffered the same fate as Lavinia.

"Maybe." Striker sniffed the air. "Do you smell peppermint?"

I thought of the *Iced Fire* I'd doused my leg in at the bookstore and felt my cheeks grow warm. I shook my head and he frowned at the air.

"So, what other motives are you looking at?" I asked innocently.

Striker disarmed me with a full smile this time. It was the first time I'd seen him smile and I realized it was quite charming.

"Oh, no ... you can't get information out of me *that* easily." He shook his head at me. "Besides I don't want you running around investigating the other motives."

"I don't need *you* to give me leads." I tilted my chin up. "I have some of my own."

"I was afraid you were going to say that. I hope I don't have to arrest you to keep you out of trouble."

I narrowed my eyes at him, not knowing if he was joking or serious. He couldn't actually arrest me, could he?

"I don't think Augusta would keep me in jail." The truth was I *wasn't* sure that she wouldn't keep me in jail—she'd warned me many times about investigating.

Striker laughed, and I was annoyed to discover his laugh was actually pleasant. "I think your sister would agree. She doesn't want you getting caught up in anything that might get you hurt. It's funny—your last name suits you to a tee."

"How's that?"

"You take a lot of chances ... unfortunately those chances could end up getting you hurt."

I almost melted a little at the concern in Striker's eyes, but I really hated it when people tried to tell me what to do and I was more than a little annoyed that it was probably true that my own sister would let me sit in jail.

"Well, maybe if you and Augusta could find the real killer, I wouldn't feel the need to take those chances," I said haughtily then swung around and started to walk away.

"Hey, Chance," he called after me, and I half-turned looking over my shoulder at him.

"What?"

"You look nice."

I spun back away from him, my heart fluttering at the compliment. Okay, maybe he was being sarcastic, but he'd actually seemed sincere.

It wasn't like me to get all flustered when someone complimented me, and that made me mad. Should I say something? I couldn't think of a snappy comeback, so I focused on keeping my eyes straight ahead while I walked away.

Chapter Eighteen

Outside the library, the weather had turned downright gloomy. Dark clouds hung overhead and the air had turned chilly. The street was dry, but it smelled like rain.

I had a few minutes to kill before Lavinia's service, so I decided to pop in and visit Pepper at *The Tea Room*.

The smell of herbal tea and cookies hit me as soon as I opened the door to Pepper's shop. The color scheme of light greens, pink and turquoise brightened the room, making me forget about the dismal weather outside. The scroll designs of the white cafe tables and chairs added whimsy to the old-fashioned setting. Petite chandeliers glittered from the ceiling, dazzling the room with soft light. The tables boasted crisp white tablecloths and napkins made from vintage fabric.

Pepper stood behind the counter at the far end of the shop. Behind her, a wide, tall shelf was stacked with various jars and bags, adorned with ribbons and filled with herbal tea.

Pepper greeted me with a smile and I started toward her, doing a double take when the person she'd been waiting on turned around.

Ophelia Withington.

I hesitated. Did I really want to talk to Ophelia? Pepper and Ophelia both stared at me expectantly and I realized I didn't have much choice. I slowed my pace, not so eager to get to the counter anymore.

"Hi, Willa," Pepper greeted me cheerfully.

Ophelia smiled at me. "Willa, so nice to see you again."

I raised a brow at her. It was?

The two other ladies turned their attention back to the purchase Ophelia was making. My gut twinged as I noticed they were laughing it up like old friends. Pepper put the purchase, which looked like a bunch of dried up leaves, twigs and sticks, into a crisp white paper bag stamped with the gold logo of *The Tea Room* and handed it across the counter to Ophelia, who grabbed the two sturdy twine handles and turned to leave.

"You girls take care, now." Ophelia waved at us graciously as she sashayed out of the shop.

"What's up with her?" I frowned at Pepper.

"She wanted to buy some of the tea we brought to her the other day."

"She did?" I turned and looked at the door through which Ophelia had disappeared.

"Yes, did you notice how pleasant she was? She's such a dear, really." Pepper leaned across the counter and whispered. "I think my tea really helped her."

"Maybe." I was still suspicious of Ophelia, and to tell the truth, not too confident in Pepper's teas either. Pepper was beaming like a lighthouse, though, and I didn't want to crush her, so I plastered a smile on my face and tried to act enthusiastic. "That's great."

Pepper turned around and plucked various herbs out of jars she had sitting open on the counter behind her. She took a pinch of this and a twig of that, placing them all into a silver ball infuser.

"Sorry I can't go to Lavinia's service with you. Camilla can't come in today and I have no one to watch the shop," she said in between pinching and plucking.

"Oh, that's okay; I need to talk to Augusta anyway about you-know-who." I jerked my head toward the door Ophelia had just exited. "So I couldn't hang around with you anyway."

Pepper poured water into a teacup and then dunked the infuser in. "Oh, you still don't think Ophelia did it, do you?"

"Well, the evidence does point to her ..."

Pepper's lips were pressed in a thin line as she bobbed the infuser up and down, turning the water in the teacup from clear to a rich mahogany. "What about the other clues?"

I tapped my finger on the counter as I thought about the other clues. The bronzes hadn't been stolen, but that didn't mean someone hadn't been trying to steal them that morning. Ophelia mentioned she'd seen a big black car, but she could be trying to cast suspicion away from her. The blue fabric on the embosser might help provide physical evidence, but I knew from my crime reporting days I'd need something else to make that stick.

"I'm trying to figure out the best way to follow up on those," I said.

Pepper slid the tea across the counter to me and I picked it up, sipping it absently, my mind on the clues. Maybe Lavinia was right and I *had* been too focused on Ophelia. The truth was, I couldn't come up with a motive for her to be in the library or to want Lavinia dead ... unless it had something to do with the lies they had both told about the church.

My mind went back to my conversation with Emma at the church—she'd seemed secretive, too ... and what had she been holding behind her back? I made a mental note to investigate the church further.

"Don't you have to get going?" Pepper nodded at the green 1930s kitchen clock on the wall and I realized Lavinia's service was going to start in ten minutes.

"Yeah, I guess I'd better."

"I bet you'll run into Eddie Striker," Pepper teased in a singsong voice.

My stomach did a flip-flop and the teacup clattered in the saucer as I put it down. I felt my cheeks burn. What was up with that? Had it been so long since I'd had a date that even the mention of a cute guy made me act like a teenager?

And come to think of it, the abrasive, annoying Sheriff Striker wasn't even all that cute.

I faux smiled at Pepper. "Funny."

My stomach felt a little queasy as I turned and started toward the door, pushing thoughts of Eddie Striker out of my mind and replacing them with ideas on how to find Lavinia's killer.

By the time I got outside, I'd forgotten all about Striker. My mind so focused on how to investigate the few clues I had, that I didn't even realize I'd sucked down the entire cup of tea.

***

The air had grown heavy with moisture and I wished I'd been smart enough to bring a raincoat. I realized ruefully that the time I'd spent that morning taming my hair had been in vain—the rain would make it go wild and it would re-arrange itself however it wanted.

I wrapped my arms around myself as I walked down the side street that led to the church.

Lavinia's family had decided on a short graveside ceremony, so I skirted the perimeter of the church to get to the graveyard behind it.

The cemetery was on a hill with the older graves at the bottom and newer ones at the top. I could already see people starting to gather about three quarters of the way up and I picked up the pace, passing the old-fashioned gravestones with their strange etchings on the way.

A mist had formed on the hill and it hung low to the ground, creating a ghostly effect that I thought was quite appropriate for Lavinia's funeral. My leg started to ache halfway up the hill and I was limping by the time I reach the site where several mourners were already gathered.

Lavinia didn't have any children or husband left living, just two sisters, their frail bodies huddled around the hole in the ground that would eventually become the final resting place of Lavinia's earthly remains. Her sisters seemed genuinely upset and I had already decided they were too frail to be considered as suspects. Was there someone else here who could be the killer?

I scanned the crowd, recognizing most of the people. It had started to drizzle and I noticed most everyone wore a raincoat or trench coat. I automatically started checking to see if any of them were navy blue.

The hearse pulled up and the dark-suited pallbearers from Stilton's Funeral parlor slid out the casket and carried it to the grave. I half expected to see Lavinia's ghost sitting on top of it, but apparently she had better things to do than attend her own funeral.

Pastor Foley appeared at the head of the grave and started talking about Lavinia. I stood off to the side, trying to gauge people's reactions. If the killer were here, would they do something that gave them away?

Most everyone had his or her head bent in prayer. I caught the eye of Bing, standing off to the side next to Cordelia, Hattie and Josiah. Apparently, Bing had recovered enough to attend the service. He nodded and bent his head, staring at his hands that were clasped in front of him. I took note of the large trench coat he wore—in tan, not navy blue.

Movement further up the hill caught my attention. The hairs on the back of my neck prickled as I saw something scurry between gravestones.

A small, furry animal ran out from the woods, making a beeline for one of the large monuments.

I watched in fascination as more furry figures came out of the woods, darting behind gravestones and making their way closer. About fifty feet away they stopped, and I saw the head of a cat peek over the top of one of the stones. I recognized it as the large feral cat Pandora had the run-in with behind the library. Beside it, a tiny face peered around the edge of the stone—the small kitten with the torn-up ear.

The cats were playing in the graveyard, watching us warily, almost as if they were attendees at the funeral.

Pastor Foley rambled on and I noticed Augusta and Striker had pulled up in Augusta's black pickup. They got out quietly and stood on the other side of the street.

Striker's eyes scanned the crowd, much like I had been doing and probably for the same reason. My heart jerked when his eyes met mine and then narrowed in suspicion before he nodded slightly and continued scanning.

I tried to keep my attention on the crowd, looking for anything suspicious, but my eyes kept sliding over to Striker, who I almost didn't recognize in his dark suit. He towered over Augusta, who looked like a midget standing beside him in her black pantsuit. I guess they didn't want to scare off the crowd by wearing police garb.

Foley finished his eulogy and the crowd started to disperse. Bing turned and made a beeline for his truck. The cats scampered into the woods. I raced over to tell Augusta about Ophelia's cape and find out why both sheriffs were here before they drove off.

On my way over, I noticed that Ophelia had been conspicuously absent from the service.

"Hey, Gus, what brings you here dressed like that?" I nodded at Augusta's outfit, sliding a sideways glance at Striker.

"Oh, just, paying our respects, same as you," Striker cut in. His suit looked like it was tailor-made. Of course, it would have to be in order to fit his broad shoulders. The dark blue color highlighted his gray eyes, making them look like slate. He looked good ... almost as good as the chocolate donut hole Augusta had slipped out of her pocket and popped into her mouth.

"So, did you guys notice anything out of place?" I asked.

Striker was right about one thing. They were here for the same reason I was, but it had more to do with detecting than paying our respects.

Striker smirked at me and my stomach started to feel queasy. "Well, you know they say the killer usually shows up at the funeral."

"So you think someone who was here did it?" I asked.

"There is one person here who keeps suspiciously popping up in the investigation," he answered.

"Really? Who?"

155

"You."

I tilted my head and fisted my hands on my hips. "Surely you don't think—"

Striker raised a brow at me and smiled that damned dimpled smile. "You sure do seem to know a lot about it."

I felt fury race through my veins, took a deep breath and was about to ream him out when Augusta interrupted.

"Willa, he's joking." She looked up at Striker and popped a jelly donut hole in her mouth. "Aren't you?"

"Yeah. Mostly. But she does keep showing up everywhere ... almost getting in the way. I warned her we might have to arrest her for her own safety." He looked down at Augusta. "Isn't that right?"

Augusta pursed her lips at me. "Yes, that *is* right. I've warned you before, Willa. Investigating on your own can be dangerous."

I shifted my weight to my right leg to ease the throbbing in my left and looked around at the dispersing crowd. Time to change the subject.

"Did you hurt your leg?" Striker asked, surprising me with the gentle tone of concern in his voice.

"Just remnants of an old accident," I said vaguely, hoping he got the hint that I didn't want to talk about it. Something flashed in his eyes—was that sympathy? I certainly didn't need his sympathy and I felt my stomach turn queasy again. I sure hoped I wasn't catching some kind of stomach bug.

"Anyway, we have to get back to work." Augusta opened the driver's door of the truck and Striker started around the back to the passenger side.

"Before you go, I have a lead I wanted to share." They both stopped and looked at me.

"What is it?" Augusta asked.

I bit my bottom lip. This might really get me in trouble with them, but I *had* to get them to investigate Ophelia's closet. "I couldn't help but notice the embosser we found in back of the library had a blue thread on it."

Augusta crossed her arms over her chest. "And?"

"Well, I happen to know that Ophelia Withington has a blue cape that looks like a color match ... and Myrna at the coffee shop said she saw Ophelia there that morning."

Augusta and Striker exchanged a look and I felt a spark of hope. Did they know something about Ophelia already?

"Also, I noticed Ophelia wasn't at the service today," I added triumphantly. Surely, her absence was a sign of guilt?

"Willa, that doesn't really mean anything," Augusta said.

"Yeah, but shouldn't you get a search warrant or something and match the fibers of the cape to that on the embosser?"

"We could, but even if they matched it wouldn't prove anything. That fiber could have been on the embosser before Lavinia was killed," Augusta said.

"And besides," Striker added, "we've already investigated Ophelia, and she has an alibi."

"She does?" My brows mashed together and I looked from Augusta to Striker.

"Yep," Augusta nodded. "An air-tight alibi. She was at the bank making a deposit and their security cameras have her time-stamped picture to prove it. According to the M.E., she was there at the exact time Lavinia died—Ophelia couldn't have killed her."

I stared at her incredulously, disappointment weighing my stomach down. I'd wasted a lot of time and energy chasing down the clues that pointed to Ophelia.

So, if Ophelia wasn't the killer ... then who was?

Chapter Nineteen

"I can't believe Ophelia has an alibi," I muttered to myself as I rolled my damp dress into a ball and threw it down on the floor in the tiny bathroom of my shop.

"Mew." Pandora pushed a paw under the door in agreement.

"I still think she's up to something." I slid on my jeans, then slipped the pink sweater over my head. A quick look in the mirror confirmed that the combination of humidity from the weather and static electricity from the sweater had made my hair frizz. I rummaged through the medicine cabinet and found an elastic band that I used to corral my shoulder-length curls into a ponytail.

Leaning closer to the mirror, I plucked out a white hair—darn things had been making an appearance in one spot at my temple and I was doing my best to avoid having a thick white stripe in my red hair.

I made my way out into the shop, turned the sign to 'Open' and brought the box of books I'd gotten from Barry to the counter so I could enter them in my computer program before I put them in their new temporary home on one of the bookshelves in the store.

Pandora slunk over and got busy sniffing and rubbing the side of her face on the box, stopping to stare up at me with round eyes every few seconds.

My mind wandered as I worked on the tedious data-entry.

"I wonder if Barry's strange fainting spell has anything to do with Lavinia's murder?" I asked out loud, squinting out into the store, hoping to see the swirly mist of Lavinia's ghost. I had questions for her.

"Meow." Pandora rubbed her cheek vigorously on the now empty box.

"You're right, that's too farfetched. There's no way they could possibly be related."

Pandora let out a low "mew" swatting in the air at something only visible to her.

"Right, I thought so. But what about Bing? Why was he driving down the road so fast?"

Pandora made a sneezing noise and shook her head.

I pictured Bing in his truck, so intent on driving that he didn't even notice me coming the other way.

"He was driving away from Barry's ... or was he driving *to* some place?" I'd seen him driving on the road that went past the turnoff to Barry's, but that didn't mean he'd been at Barry's. He could have been coming from further up the mountain. And where had he been driving *to*?

I finished cataloguing the books and hit the button to print the price tags for each book. The printer hummed to life, startling Pandora and causing her to jump sideways and hiss at it. I couldn't help but laugh … that printer got her every time.

I grabbed the stickers and shoved them in my back pocket, then lifted a stack of half the books and headed out toward the row of bookcases where I kept the children's books, Pandora trotting obediently at my heels.

"There's still that strange secret at the church that Lavinia and Ophelia both seemed to share. Even though Ophelia has an alibi, I think that's worth checking into."

I hoped Lavinia would show up and clue me in herself, but ghosts hardly ever appeared when you wanted them to. They liked to show up when they were least expected and scare the bejesus out of you, instead.

I slapped the price tags on the children's books and slid them into their slots, then headed to the section where I kept the classics.

"So, the only real clues I have are the black car Ophelia saw and the bronzes," I said, still talking to Pandora, who I'd like to think was hanging onto my every word.

"Meow," she said as if to encourage me.

"I have no idea how to start investigating the big black car." I put the prices on the three books I had left in my arms and found a place for each of them on the bookshelf. "As for the bronzes, I know exactly where to start."

***

I closed up the shop promptly at five, locking Pandora inside despite her belligerent howls. Guilt ate away at me as I headed out of town and up the mountain, but it was for her own good. She never stayed put in the car and I just couldn't bring her with me this time. I was going to start my inquiries about the bronzes at the source and I didn't need to be chasing my cat around the Bates estate if she decided to take off and run wild.

The humid fog had turned to drizzle. Dark clouds rolled in along the valley as I drove the winding mountain road to the Bates mansion. I passed the cutoff to Barry's and wondered if I should check in on him in case he had had another fainting spell, but thought better of it. He was a grown man and didn't need me looking after him.

The Bates mansion cut into the side of the mountain—an immense old estate. The granite house boasted four stories, complete with million-dollar views from every window. An imposing black iron gate surrounded the main buildings. Thankfully, it was open and I drove my Jeep up the crushed gravel driveway, which circled around a giant fountain in front of the house.

I couldn't say the house was friendly. The gray stone was cold and the oak door with black, cast-iron hinges looked like something you'd see in a medieval castle. A black iron fence ran along the roofline, its posts stabbing angrily up into the sky.

I slid out of the Jeep, my stomach twisting and my leg burning as I approached the gothic wood door. I pushed the doorbell and felt a twinge of panic.

Maybe I should have planned what to say first?

The door glided open and a man in what looked like butler garb stood in front of me.

"Yes?" He quirked an eyebrow at my frizzy hair and faded jeans.

"I'd like to talk to Idris Bates, please."

He stiffly stepped aside and gestured for me to enter.

"I'll see if Mr. Bates is available," he said, then glided off down the hall.

Did the Bates' really have an honest to goodness butler? As I looked around the foyer, the word 'opulent' came to mind. The shiny, travertine marble floor reflected light from the giant crystal chandelier that hung in the center of the round entryway. To the right, a carved mahogany staircase wound its way upstairs. To the left, french doors led into another room. In front of me was a round table with a whopper of a flower arrangement on it.

Were those flowers real? I reached out to touch one...

"Can I help you?"

I jerked my hand back and spun around to see Derek Bates standing behind me.

"Hi, Derek," I smiled. "I was actually coming to talk to your grandfather."

"Grandfather is napping. He's rather old, you know. Needs his sleep." Derek's words were clipped, not like his usual friendly self. Maybe the Bates' family didn't like it so much when people came to see them unannounced.

He stood in the same spot, making no move to invite me in further. I tilted my head to the side to see the room behind him. It seemed to be some sort of library. He raised a brow and looked at me expectantly.

I cleared my throat. "I ... umm ... I was coming to ask your grandfather about some bronzes he donated to the library many years ago."

Derek narrowed his eyes. "Bronzes ... oh, yes. We have a big collection. I don't remember him donating any to the library, though."

"It was in the sixties, before our time," I said, remembering that even though the family trait of a thick streak of premature gray in Derek's hair made him *seem* a lot older, he was really only a few years my senior. He would have been a kid when the bronzes were donated.

Derek chuckled, relaxing a bit. "Ahh ... what did you want to know?"

"I was wondering if your grandfather would remember who was around at the ceremony when he donated them."

"Why would you want to know that?"

"We think someone might have broken into the library to steal them and I was trying to figure out who might have known they were there. They were moved downstairs years ago and I think most everyone has forgotten about them."

"We?" Derek's smile faltered and he looked at me funny. "Are you working with the police or something?"

I shifted uneasily. "Well, no, it's just—"

Crash!

We both swiveled toward the sound that had come from the room on the left.

Derek's face took on a look of panic and we started toward the room, only to be met by Felicity Bates, Derek's mother, who swept out of the room in a long black dress, wide sleeves flowing around her wrists.

She stopped short at the sight of us, a look of surprise on her face.

"Mother, what's going on?" Derek's voice was tinged with panic.

"Oh, dear, I was just practicing ..." Felicity let her voice trail off as she noticed me standing there. "What is she doing here?"

My brows shot up. She didn't sound very friendly. "I just came to ask—"

"She was just leaving," Derek interrupted me, grabbing my elbow roughly and jerking me toward the door.

"Was that a crash?" Derek's brother Carson came running down the stairs, taking them two at a time. "Mother, are you okay?"

"Yes, but there's a mess in there." Felicity pointed toward the french doors and Carson looked in that direction, catching sight of me on the way.

"Oh. Hi, Willa." His eyes went to Derek's hand on my elbow and he shot me a confused and apologetic look.

"Hi, Carson—" Derek cut off my words by tugging me forcefully in the direction of the door. I turned, looking back over my shoulder at Carson, then craning to see what was going on in the room beyond the french doors. I couldn't see a thing, though, and the movement was making my leg hurt.

Derek pulled the front door open with one hand, and shoved me through the threshold backwards. Inside the house, I could see Felicity gesturing wildly to Carson about something. Carson was making soothing motions, I assumed to calm her down. I looked at Derek.

"Hey, wait. I—"

Derek slammed the door in my face and I stumbled backward. I could feel my bad leg starting to give out on me and I braced for the impact of the cold, granite steps, screwing my face up into a grimace and flapping my arms.

But, instead of feeling the sharp edge of the hard rock steps, I found myself in a pair of strong arms. I twisted around, my heart thudding against my rib cage and looked straight into the steely gray eyes of ... Eddie Striker.

Chapter Twenty

"What are *you* doing here?" I asked through pain-clenched teeth.

"I should be asking the same of you." He looked up at the imposing oak door. "What did you do to him to make him slam the door on you like that?"

"Nothing," I said, although not with as much indignation as I'd intended, because I was distracted by his woodsy, leathery smell. I probably smelled like medicinal peppermint.

"So, what *are* you doing here?" He gently eased me back up onto my feet.

Instead of answering, I gingerly tested my left leg, wincing in pain as I increased the pressure.

Striker's face turned hard. "Did he hurt you?"

"No, the weather makes it act up." Of course, Derek's forceful exit didn't help any, but I didn't need Striker getting all macho and defending me.

"Where does it hurt?"

I pointed to where it hurt, an area on the side, running mid-thigh to mid-calf. He knelt down, poking and prodding at the area, causing me to yip and groan at various decibels, depending on how much it hurt. He was surprisingly gentle, but even the slightest pressure was painful.

After a few minutes, he stood up. I shook my leg out, surprised to find it actually felt a little better.

"The muscle is knotted up. Probably from previous damage ... you mentioned you were in a car accident ..."

"Yes, a little over a year ago."

"You should be getting massages, maybe even acupuncture." He looked down at my leg. "That would help it heal quicker and give you less pain."

"Oh, thanks." I wasn't sure what to say. Why was he suddenly being so nice, and how did he know so much about muscle pain?

His head was tilted, still looking down at my leg. The drizzle had stopped and the late afternoon sun made an appearance from behind the clouds. I noticed how the angle of the light accentuated his chiseled features, making him look dangerously handsome. My stomach started to flip-flop uncomfortably and I took a step away.

"You didn't answer my question." Striker's eyes followed me as I slowly backed toward my car. "What were you doing here, and why was Derek throwing you out?"

"He wasn't actually throwing me out." I pressed my lips together, puzzled as to why he did throw me out. "There was a crash in one of the rooms and I guess they needed to clean it up."

Striker looked at me like he didn't believe me.

I half-shrugged and spread my arms. "I know it sounds weird, but it's true. Why are you here?"

"Police business."

No kidding. I wondered if he was following the same trail that I was. "About the bronzes?"

Striker narrowed his eyes at me. "Maybe."

We stood there staring at each other for a few electrically charged seconds while I decided whether to keep badgering him for information or just leave.

He must have been thinking the same thing, because he said, "I get the impression you're not going to stop looking into this. Maybe it would be best if we compared notes. How about we meet back at the *The Mystic Cafe* in say ... fifteen minutes?"

Compare notes? Since when did the police want to let me in on their investigation? He must have thought I had some information he could use ... but maybe he had some *I* could use.

My pulse kicked into high gear and I heard myself say, "Sounds good. I have to go back to town before I go home anyway."

"Okay, I'll only be a few minutes here. Order me a small coffee. Black." Striker turned to the door and I hobbled to my Jeep, wondering if I'd just accepted an invitation that was finally going to give me a break in the case ... or that would lead to our first date.

***

I found a parking spot on Main Street between my shop and the Mystic Cafe. Glancing over to the bookstore, I could see Pandora glaring at me from her cat bed in the window. Her displeasure was obvious in her slitted golden-green orbs and I wondered if she'd demonstrate it to me by leaving a hairball on my purple sofa ... or worse.

It was just a little after five and the cafe was fairly empty. I chose a booth near the back and sat facing the door. I ordered Striker his coffee and one for myself, along with a roast beef and melted Swiss cheese on an onion roll. I was hungry.

Striker strolled in just as the sandwich appeared on the table.

"Roast beef and Swiss?" He eyed the sandwich before taking a sip of the coffee I'd shoved over to his side of the table.

"You want half?" I raised my brow at him and slid the sandwich toward him.

"No, thanks." He watched me smear some horseradish from the condiment dish on the sandwich and take a bite. I suddenly felt self-conscious, my face flushing—probably from the horseradish. I swallowed and the food sat like a leaden lump in my stomach.

"So, what have you got?" I asked.

"You go first."

I shrugged. "I don't really have anything. My best guess is that it has something to do with the bronzes."

"How did you find out about the bronzes, anyway?"

"Josiah Barrows, the old postmaster mentioned it. He remembered when they were donated." No way was I going to tell him Lavinia had verified that.

"So that's why you were at the Bates'?"

I shrugged.

"And how did you happen to be behind the library, conveniently finding the murder weapon?"

"Aha! So that *was* the murder weapon."

Striker nodded. "We found Lavinia's blood on it. But how did you even know to look there?"

I narrowed my eyes. I didn't like how this was going. It was starting to feel more like an interrogation than sharing information. So far, it was all take and no give.

"I actually wasn't there because I thought I would find a murder weapon. At that time, I didn't even know Lavinia had been murdered. I was looking for my cat," I said, then tried to turn the tide so I was the one getting information instead of giving it. "So, you were at the Bates mansion because of the bronzes, too? That must mean you think the same thing I do."

"Not necessarily. But I have to follow every lead."

I took another bite of my sandwich. A string of cheese dribbled down my chin, causing the corners of Striker's mouth to curl up in an alarmingly charming grin. I swiped at the cheese with as much dignity as I could. "Have you and Augusta come up with any other clues, besides the embosser and the bronzes?"

Striker studied me, probably deciding if he could trust me. I stared back with my most earnest look. It must have worked, because he said, "We did find some gray hairs clutched in Lavinia's hand."

My brows shot up. "Gray hairs? You mean like from an old person?"

Striker shrugged. "Or a young person with gray hair."

My eyes immediately looked up at my hairline where those pesky white hairs were starting to appear. I noticed Striker looking, too.

"Mine are white," I said.

Striker laughed. "You hardly have any—this was a clump."

"So you think she grabbed onto the killer's hair?" I made a mental note to ask Lavinia about that.

"It's possible."

"Maybe it was her own hair. She did have gray hair." Like half the town, I thought, as I looked around the half-empty cafe noticing most of the patrons were senior citizens.

"It's not a match with her hair." Striker rubbed his chin. "Unfortunately, the forensics lab here doesn't have all the latest equipment, so we couldn't tell much more about it. Augusta sent it out for more analysis, but that's going to take a while."

Striker watched patiently while I polished off my sandwich. He'd given me a clue and now I supposed I should reciprocate.

I wiped my mouth with the brown paper napkin. "Ophelia said she saw a long, black car speeding away from town that morning."

Striker's left brow lifted a fraction of an inch and I realized with satisfaction the he hadn't known about that.

"You talked to her?" he asked.

"Yep. She said she saw the car after she did her banking." I paused. "Didn't you say she was at the bank at Lavinia's time of death?"

Striker nodded. "I suppose that could have been the killer making a hasty get-away. Did she see who was driving?"

I shook my head.

He pressed his lips together. "Hmm … well that's something to keep in mind, anyway."

"It doesn't seem like there's much to go on." My words were weighted down with disappointment. How were we ever going to find Lavinia's killer with these skimpy clues? "I mean, there are so many people that each of these clues could point to."

"I know it seems that way." Striker finished his coffee and made 'getting ready to leave' motions. "But the trick is to find the one person that all the clues fall into place for. So, if you come up with any others, let me know ... it could mean the difference between narrowing things down to the real killer or not."

He pushed up from the table and I followed suit, all the while thinking about the big ring Lavinia had said the killer was wearing. Glancing around the shop, I picked out several people who had big rings on. Like the other clues, it wasn't much to go on and I couldn't tell Striker about it anyway ... not unless I wanted to tell him I talked to ghosts. Which I didn't.

Striker swiped up my sandwich wrappings and paper cup and tossed them in the trash, then opened the door for me and we stepped out onto the street. It was dusk, but the clouds had dispersed and a setting slice of sun glittered cheerfully on the street.

"I'm parked down there." Striker pointed down the street, and I could see the police car a few spots past my shop.

"I have to go that way, too," I said, starting in that direction. "Gotta stop in the shop and pick up my cat."

Striker fell in beside me and I was suddenly awkwardly aware of his presence. He was walking kind of close, which, I noticed with annoyance, made my pulse skitter.

I tried to stick to business. "So, what made you share the clues with me?"

Striker snorted. "It was obvious you weren't going to stop looking into this, so I figured it was better to join forces so I could keep an eye on you."

"Are you sure it's not because you thought I had some clues you couldn't figure out?" I teased.

Striker laughed, and his wide smile made my stomach flip. We'd reached my shop and he stopped beside me on the sidewalk as I dug around in my pocket for the key.

"Well, thanks for sharing." I turned toward the door and he touched my arm, turning me back to him.

I looked up at him. His face had turned serious. "Willa, I want you to be very careful on this. Don't go off on any investigations without talking to me first. We still don't know the motive for this killing and ... well ... it could dangerous."

His gray eyes turned dark with feeling and my mouth dried up.

"Okay," I croaked.

His grip on my arm tightened and he pulled me a little closer. I held my breath, my stomach tossing the roast beef sandwich around like the *Andrea Gail* in The Perfect Storm.

Was he going to kiss me?

He dipped his head toward mine.

And that's when I threw up on his shoes.

Chapter Twenty-One

"You threw up on his shoes?" Pepper stared at me, her emerald eyes as big as saucers.

"Yeah, I think I might be coming down with something, although I feel fine now." I pressed my fingertips against my temple in a futile attempt to make the painful pounding stop. "Other than this headache."

"What happened?" She busied herself behind the counter of her shop, getting things ready for the morning crowd, glancing up at me every so often as I told her how I'd run into Striker at the Bates mansion. Her lips quirked up in a smug smile when I told her about how we'd had coffee and exchanged clues.

"His car was parked up here, so we were standing in front of my shop while I dug out my key." I leaned across the counter, lowering my voice even though no one was in the shop to hear me. "It almost seemed like he was about to kiss me."

I had Pepper's full attention. "Really? What happened?"

"I felt sick and threw up. Lucky thing he was wearing police issue shoes—they should clean off pretty easily."

"That sounds awful … what did he do?"

"He was a complete gentleman," I said, grimacing at the memory. "He acted like it was nothing. But I noticed he didn't seem like he wanted to kiss me anymore after that. It was humiliating … took me three Appletini's to recover.

"Maybe that explains the headache I have this morning. Funny thing though, I didn't feel sick when I was drinking those."

"Oh, dear," Pepper wrung her hands together, her eyes darting around the store as if she was trying to avoid eye contact with me.

"Pepper, do you have something to tell me?" I didn't like the way she was *not* looking at me.

"Well …" she wrinkled her face. "I was only trying to help …"

"You didn't!" My heart dropped—had she given me one of her crazy herbal teas thinking she could fix me up with Striker?

Pepper nodded. "I guess maybe I shouldn't have made it a love-*sick* potion."

"Pepper! I asked you not to." I gave her a 'how-could-you' look, but the stricken look on her face made it impossible for me to be too mad at her. "So now I'm going to get sick whenever I see Striker? Did you give him a tea, too?"

"No, he didn't need one." Pepper tucked a long strand of hair back into the swirly bun on top of her head. "But don't worry, I'll make this right.

I felt a moment of panic as she turned around and started throwing herbs into an infuser. Her previous tea had made me throw up, who knew what this one would do to me?

I held my hands up in front of me. "Oh, no. I'm not drinking another tea from you. Not with the way those things backfire. Besides, it's probably for the best if I throw up every time I see Striker. The last thing I need is to get involved with him."

Pepper stopped what she was doing and turned to me, her hands on her hips. "Actually, Willa, I think you do need to get involved. How long since you and Jake split up?"

My heart twisted at the thought of my ex-husband. Our break-up hadn't been pretty. "Two years."

"Right, so it's about time you got interested in someone else. I'm not saying you have to marry the guy, but go out and have some fun, at least. You don't want to end up a shriveled up old maid, do you?"

Did I? The thought didn't seem all that unappealing if it meant I could avoid another heartbreak.

"I'll think about it," I said, mostly to get her to stop talking about it. "I did find out a new clue, though."

"When you were at the Bates mansion?"

"No, but come to think of it something strange happened there."

"What?"

"I was talking to Derek and there was a big crash. Felicity came out of a side room and then everyone got all weird and Derek rushed me out of there."

Pepper's brow creased. "Did Felicity drop something?"

"I'm not sure." I chewed my lower lip trying to remember what she'd said. "She said something strange ... that she was practicing something. Maybe she does karate or something."

"Or maybe she was practicing her spells and they went haywire." Pepper looked at me out of the corner of her eye as she dunked the infuser in the hot water she'd poured into a teacup.

"Spells?" I wrinkled my face up at her.

"Some people say she's some kind of witch." Pepper slid the teacup across the counter at me and I eyed it suspiciously, wondering what might happen to me if I drank it. Would it cure me of throwing up on Striker, or simply cause me some other embarrassing malady?

"That's silly." I lifted the cup to my lips and sniffed. It smelled like mushrooms and dirt. "There's no such thing as witches."

Pepper simply shrugged and I thought back to my conversation with Elspeth about magic. I'd never been one to believe in magic or paranormal activity ... but that was *before* I started talking to ghosts.

"So what was the clue?" Pepper prompted.

"Oh, right." I took a tentative sip of tea. It was actually pretty good. "Striker said they found some gray hairs clutched in Lavinia's hand."

"From the killer?"

"Presumably. Although, we don't know for sure. I plan to ask Lavinia if she remembers pulling her killer's hair."

Pepper's lips curled in a triumphant smile. "So the killer couldn't have been Ophelia."

"No, you were right. It's not her. She has an airtight alibi." I told her about the time-stamped photo of Ophelia at the bank.

"I knew it!" Pepper snapped her fingers. "So now you can narrow your list down to just people with gray hair."

"We don't know that hair was from the killer, and anyway, that still leaves quite a long list of people."

"Yeah, but I have a good idea where you can start." Pepper thrust her chin in the direction of the window.

Outside, Cordelia, Hattie, Bing and Josiah were strolling by, Styrofoam coffee cups in hand, on their way to my bookstore. My stomach dropped as I realized they all had gray hair.

***

I jogged the short distance from Pepper's shop to my bookstore where Bing, Cordelia, Hattie and Josiah were huddled together in conversation outside my door. Could one of them be the killer?

Of course not … I hoped. These people were my friends. I'd practically grown up with them. It just wasn't possible one of them had killed Lavinia.

"Hey, Willa," Bing said as they parted to let me open the door.

We filed inside and Hattie handed me a coffee. I leaned against my front counter, watching them settle on the purple sofa as I sipped the coffee slowly. The tea that Pepper gave me had already given me a boost and I didn't need the caffeine as much as usual.

"That was a lovely service for Lavinia yesterday," Cordelia said.

"Did you go, Willa?" Hattie raised a white brow at me.

"I did," I answered. "I saw you over on the side, but you guys left and I had to talk to Augusta about something."

"Oh?" Bing glanced up from his coffee. "About the murder?"

"Sort of." I didn't want to get into the whole thing about how I'd suspected Ophelia now that she'd been cleared.

"Seems to me that anyone who would be so bold as to try to steal those bronzes must have some big money problems," Hattie said.

Cordelia nodded. "I imagine the police are looking into that."

"Well, I hope they're making some progress," Hattie said. "It's disturbing to know there is a killer in our midst."

"*Are* they making progress?" Josiah asked, his eyes boring into mine.

"I'm not sure. You know how little Augusta tells me." I chewed on my bottom lip. Josiah had been the postmaster his whole life. Surely, he didn't make a ton of money in his retirement. And he was one of the few people that remembered about the bronzes and knew their value.

My stomach clenched. Surely, I wasn't suspecting Josiah ... was I? I caught myself looking at his hands to see if he wore a big ring. He didn't ... at least he wasn't wearing one *today*.

Bing closed the plastic tab on the lid of his coffee and stood up. I noticed that he *was* wearing a big ring. His Magician's Guild ring—he always wore it. I reminded myself that lots of people wore big rings, especially class rings and rings from organizations.

"What if it wasn't the bronzes? What if they were after something else?" Bing said. His eyes held mine and I got the impression he was trying to tell me something. Or warn me.

Cordelia, Hattie and Josiah swiveled their faces toward Bing.

Cordelia's forehead took on another layer of wrinkles. "What else would they be looking for? The only other thing in there is books."

"That's right," Hattie said, pushing herself up from the couch. "Unless there is something else of value that the killer knows about and we don't."

Josiah tilted his head. "That could be. Seems like this is getting to be more and more of a mystery."

"It sure is," I said.

Cordelia and Josiah stood up and the four of them made their way to the door.

"See you tomorrow, Willa," Cordelia said.

"Bye," Hattie turned and waved.

"See ya," Bing nodded.

"Later," Josiah said as he shut the door behind him, leaving me alone in the bookstore.

Well, almost alone ... Lavinia's ghost swirled into view as soon as the door was firmly shut.

"So, how was my funeral?"

"It was nice. I'm surprised you weren't there." I got to the bottom of my coffee and tossed the cup in the trash.

"Oh, it's kind of tacky to show up at your own funeral." Lavinia looked at me as if she was surprised I wasn't up on the latest ghost etiquette. "So how does it look on finding my killer?"

"Well, it wasn't Ophelia," I said.

"Oh, that's too bad." Lavinia made a face. "I mean, I figured it wasn't, but still, I would have liked it to have been her. We didn't get along."

"But I did find a new clue that I need your help with."

"Oh?" Lavinia's ghostly brows swirled upwards.

"The police found some gray hairs clutched in your hand. They think you might have pulled them from the killer," I said. "Do you remember pulling out the hair of the person that pushed you?"

"Let me think ... I was walking toward the back of the stairs. I saw a shadow, then felt the pain in the back of my head. Then someone pushed me, right at the top of my back ... I flailed my arms, grabbing out for anything to keep from falling." Lavinia looked up at the ceiling, screwing her face up in thought. "Yes! I remember reaching out and grabbing on as I was falling. I heard a grunt. A few hairs ripped out. And then I fell."

A prickle of excitement rippled through my stomach. "You heard a grunt? Did you recognize who it sounded like?"

Lavinia shook her head, her shoulders drooping. "No, sorry. It was just an odd grunt. It

187

sounded like a man, though … most definitely a man."

"Well, I guess that narrows it down some." My head was starting to throb and my leg was aching. I glanced at the clock, my stomach sinking when I realized the day was just beginning. I made a mental note not to drink so many Appletini's on a work night.

"Willa?" Lavinia pulled me out of my thoughts.

"Yes?"

"I don't want to rush you, but I feel it's urgent that you step up the investigation."

I felt a tinge of annoyance. Who was *she* to be so pushy? "Oh, sorry I'm not investigating fast enough. I do have a business to run, you know."

"There's no need to get snippy. I'm simply telling you this for your own good."

"My own good? What does *your* murder have to do with my good?"

Lavinia looked confused. "I'm not sure, but ever since I died, I get these feelings and that's what I feel. Besides if you want to get rid of me, you need to find the killer."

I pressed my lips together and stared at her. I sure *did* want to get rid of her. Having ghosts pop up when you least expected them was annoying. It was enough just to have Frost and Pierce lurking in the store. They didn't seem like they were ever going to leave, and I didn't want to add any more perpetual ghosts to the mix.

"You have all these clues now and you *were* a top notch crime journalist," Lavinia pointed out. "How hard can it be to figure out who it is?"

"Right. Should be child's play," I said, feeling a sinking sensation in my stomach. "All I have to do is find a gray-haired man wearing a big ring and a blue cape that has financial trouble *and* doesn't have an alibi for the time you were killed."

Chapter Twenty-Two

The day went by quickly and I pulled into my driveway that night, exhausted from my Appletini hangover.

As usual, Pandora raced me to the farmer's porch, stopping short at a large box that blocked the path to the door.

"Mew!" She looked up at me as if it was the most important box in the world.

"What is that?" I bent down to read the note on top of the box.

Willa, here are the books I picked up for you - Enjoy! Maggie.

With everything that was going on, I'd forgotten that Maggie had the books for me. She must have returned from her buying trip and dropped them off. I made a mental note to call her and thank her as I opened the door and pushed the box inside.

Glaring at the bottle of vodka on the counter, I rummaged in the fridge for supper. I didn't have much, but managed to dig up a jar of jalapeños, shredded cheese and spaghetti sauce. I piled them on top of a toasted English muffin and then set it under the broiler to melt the cheese while I filled Pandora's bowl.

I pulled the muffin out from under the broiler before I caught the house on fire and settled at the kitchen table to eat it. My leg had started aching again. I grabbed some *Iced Fire* and rubbed it in while I waited for the muffin to cool.

Pandora sniffed in my direction, made a sour face, then trotted over to the box of books where the smell must have been more to her liking, judging by the way her nose was getting familiar with it.

I took a bite of the muffin, savoring the contrast of the creamy melted cheese and the spicy hot jalapeño. The muffin was toasted perfectly to add just the right amount of crunch.

I thought about my clues and suspects as I ate, my spirits sinking as I realized I didn't really have much of a list.

The killer had worn a cape or loose coat and had a big ring and gray hair.

A long, black car had been seen racing out of town that morning.

Valuable bronzes were in the library, so the motive could have been financial.

Who needed financial help? Maybe that was the best place to start. But the killer also had to have had means, motive and opportunity.

I hated to suspect my old friends, but Bing and Josiah both knew the value of those bronzes. Bing had said he didn't remember they were in the library, but he had been acting suspicious and it was weird that I'd seen him driving so strangely when I was going to Barry's. Once again, I wondered if Barry's passing out had anything to do with this case.

Both Bing and Josiah had gray hair. Bing wore a large ring. I didn't know if Josiah or Bing had a navy blue cape, but Bing certainly had lots of capes he used for his magician act.

I knew they were both in the area that morning because I'd seen them at my shop. Could one of them have killed Lavinia and then been so cold as to join the rest of us for coffee only an hour later?

I sighed in frustration. I hated the thought it could be one of them, but I had to explore all the angles.

"Mew." Pandora must have really liked that box because she had hopped inside and was pawing around at the books.

"Hey, don't mess those up." I pulled the box closer to me and peeked inside. The books looked interesting and I needed something to take my mind off the murder investigation.

I reached in and pulled out a book, turning it to look at the cover. *Gone With the Wind*. I opened it eagerly looking for the publication information. Most copies of the book weren't worth much, but if it was a first edition, it could be worth a lot. Just my luck, it wasn't.

I put it on the table and reached back down into the box. Pandora tried to slow me down by jumping in and out of the box while I was trying to pick a book out.

I grabbed one book that was longer than the others were, making a face when I realized what it was. A photo album. They were virtually worthless —no one wanted to buy someone else's photos, but they *were* kind of fun to look at.

Pandora must have liked it because she rubbed her face on the edge as I flipped it open. I turned to the first page and my heart skipped. Staring me in the face was a younger version of Idris Bates.

I flipped through the book, which must have been twenty years old. There were pictures of a smiling Felicity and Gardner Bates—Derek and Carson's father—in happier times. There were pictures of Derek and Carson in their twenties, and a nice picture of Idris, Gardner, Carson and Derek all with their hands on a plaque. I squinted at the picture ... it looked like a family crest. Something about the picture niggled at my mind, but before I had too much time to think about it, Pandora distracted me by jumping into my lap and pawing at the book.

"Hey, don't rip the pages." I pushed her away and she jumped back to the ground with an angry meow, then resumed her box sniffing routine. I remembered Derek had come by the bookstore looking for family scrapbooks and albums his mother might have sold by mistake at their yard sale—this must have been one of them.

I'd have to take a trip up to the Bates mansion and return it. Maybe this time and I could talk to Idris about the bronzes. My natural curiosity was piqued about Felicity and the big crash that had made Derek rush me out of the house. Maybe I could find out what, exactly, she'd been practicing.

I put the photo album on the table and looked through the rest of the box to see if there were any more Bates scrapbooks or albums. I didn't find any, but I did see some interesting books that looked to be very early editions.

I picked one out and settled back in the chair, excitement causing my pulse to pick up speed. Early books were rare and could be worth a lot of money. I opened the book, carefully fingering the thin, yellowed pages. I could see foxing—brown stains of water damage—on the edges. That would affect the value, but the book had gorgeous, hand colored plates inside that would make up for it.

Pandora got bored with sniffing the box while I was studying the book. She trotted over to the living room and started to bat around one of her cat toys. The toy made a familiar jingling noise that stirred a memory, stealing my attention from the book I'd been studying.

I'd heard that noise somewhere else recently—where?

It came to me in a snap. Emma had been hiding something that made a similar noise behind her back at the church.

Emma had gray hair.

Emma had mentioned the church's desperate need for money.

Lavinia had some sort of secret that had to do with the church.

"Could Emma be the killer?" I said out loud.

"Meow!" Pandora went crazy, throwing the ball up in the air and pouncing on it. It was almost as if she was trying to tell me something. Too bad I had no idea what that something was.

"It doesn't seem like she would be the killer."

"Mew." Pandora stopped her antics and stared at me. I picked her up and cuddled her in my lap, stroking her soft fur.

"Little old ladies don't clobber other little old ladies and push them down the stairs, do they?"

Pandora answered by purring and kneading her razor sharp claws into my arm.

I didn't know what that meant, but I did know one thing ... I was going to pay Emma a visit and find out why both Lavinia and Ophelia had lied about lighting candles at the church and what—if anything—that had to do with Lavinia's murder.

Chapter Twenty-Three

The next morning, I contemplated my plan of attack over peanut butter toast. I wanted to visit Emma at the church and find out Lavinia's secret and I also wanted to take the photo album to the Bates' and, hopefully, to find out about the bronzes.

The problem was that I didn't want to leave the shop closed too long. I'd been opening late, taking a long lunch and leaving early a lot lately and I didn't want to put customers off. Lavinia might have been murdered, but I still had to earn a living.

I decided to visit the Bates' during lunch and the church later in the afternoon. I didn't usually get too many customers after three, so I'd close early and still be able to get to the church before Emma went home for the night.

I finished my toast, eyeing Pandora who was lounging lazily on the sofa in the living room. It was probably best for me to leave her here, since I'd be in and out of the shop all day.

I opened the drawer where I kept the catnip and Pandora immediately jerked her head up, her eyes slitting open and zoning in on the drawer. She leaped down from the couch and padded over.

I took a pinch of dried herbs out of the catnip bag and sprinkled it on the floor. She sniffed, then made a gleeful meow and threw herself on her back, rubbing and rolling in the pile of herbs.

I stuffed one of her favorite toys full of the catnip and threw it. She sprang up, pouncing sideways and sliding into the wall, then scurried over to the toy, grabbing it in her mouth, tossing it in the air and catching it.

Satisfied that she was happily distracted, I grabbed the Bates' photo album and made a run for the Jeep.

**

I got to the bookstore late and the regulars were waiting for me outside. I let them in and we had the usual conversation. Bing stayed behind when Hattie, Cordelia and Josiah got up to leave.

"I was wondering if you've gotten any good books in." Bing craned his neck to look behind the counter where I usually stacked the new books. "I'm starting up a collection of old leather-bounds. The older the better."

"Well, I got some books from Barry and there were few old ones in there." I pointed toward the aisle where I kept the older books. "All my older ones would be over there."

"Great." Bing headed in that direction. He was an avid reader and liked to compile collections of antiques and then, eventually, sell them off. I guess it was an interesting way to make money out of a hobby.

The morning was filled with a whirlwind of customers and Bing must have left without a purchase as I never saw him again. I was distracted, waiting on customers and anxious to close up for lunch and get out to the Bates mansion.

I took the opportunity of the lunchtime lull to close up shop so I could take the photo album up to the Bates'. We didn't have drive-thru's in Mystic Notch, so I had to settle for eating a packet of cheese crackers that I picked up at the gas station.

I was just finishing the last one when I pulled into the Bates' crushed gravel driveway. The crackers settled like lead in my stomach as I looked at the foreboding mansion, remembering how Derek had rushed me out the last time I was there.

Maybe I wouldn't be welcome?

Glancing at the photo album on the seat beside me, I realized that was silly. Of course I would be welcome—Derek wanted the photo album. He'd made a special trip to my shop to ask about it.

Still, I felt the tingle of nerves bloom in my stomach as I walked up the steps. The four-story mansion loomed over me, sucking all the sunlight out of the day.

It was chilly and grew even cooler in the shadow of the house. A shiver tickled my spine as I pressed the fancy white porcelain doorbell.

I waited.

The sound of the bell echoed through the house, but no one came to the door. Where was the fancy butler?

Maybe I should give him more time. The house was gigantic and if he was at the other end it would take a while to get to the door.

I waited, tapping my fingertips on the soft leather of the photo album.

No one came.

Impatience spread through me. My leg started throbbing. Was no one home? I'd come all the way out here and I hoped it wasn't a wasted trip.

I backed down the steps and looked up at the house. No signs of life. Sighing, I turned back toward the driveway when a movement over by the garage caught my eye.

Was someone there? I remembered Derek liked to tinker with cars. I took off in that direction.

The gravel crunched under my feet as I approached the garage, which was almost as big as my house. Made from the same granite block as the mansion, it had two stories and four garage bays. Three of them were closed, their green wooden doors blocking what was inside. The fourth stood open, revealing a white 1960s Triumph convertible.

I approached tentatively, wrinkling my nose at the smell of oil and metal. It was dark inside and I didn't see a soul. What was that movement I'd seen?

"Hello?" I ventured.

Clunk.

"Ouch!"

Derek slid halfway out from under the Triumph on a dolly. Rubbing his head, he frowned at me from his upside down position, then recognition lit his face.

"Willa! What are you doing here?" He slid all the way out, stood up and brushed the dirt from his blue mechanic's outfit.

"I thought you might like this." I held out the photo album and he pulled a rag from his pocket, using it to wipe the grease off his hands before taking the album.

A smile formed on his lips as he leafed through the book. "Well, I'll be…"

A noise came out of the dark recesses of the garage, startling both of us. Derek swung around toward it. Carson appeared, seemingly out of nowhere, a boyish grin on his face.

He casually crossed the other bays toward us, his hands in his pockets. My eyes had adjusted to the dark and I noticed a car occupied each of the bays. A Mini-Cooper in one, a pickup truck in another, and a long dark sedan, almost like a limousine in the last. I remembered seeing Felicity being chauffeured around by a driver and noticed some dark chauffeur's coats and caps hanging on knobs at the other end of the garage. Must be nice to have money.

"Carson, jeez, do you have to sneak up on us like that?" Derek closed the album and glared at his brother. I wondered if they didn't get along ... they always seemed to before.

"Hi, Willa," Carson said, ignoring his brother, his gaze falling on the photo album. "What's that?"

"An old family photo album I came across in my travels. Thought you guys might want it."

Carson came closer.

"Let's see." He held his hand out and practically had to wrestle it away from Derek. "I hope we didn't rush you out of here the other night ... mother can be a little overzealous in her ... umm ... experiments.

"What kind of experiments is she doing?" I felt my brows creep up my forehead. Experiments?

Derek shot a look at Carson, who was busy flipping the pages of the photo album.

"Oh, yoga and stuff ... you know." Derek waved a hand dismissively.

"These are great." Carson held the book up with one hand spreading the pages apart to show the picture of the two brothers with their father and grandfather. "Look at this great picture of us with Dad and and Grandpa. Cripes, this album must be twenty-five years old."

"Yes, well, we don't need to keep Willa. I'm sure she's busy." Derek snatched the book away from Carson, who looked hurt.

"Where'd you get it?" Carson asked.

"It was in a box of books I acquired."

"Were there any other books of ours in with it?" Carson nodded toward the house. "Mother sold off some of our collection of older books and we'd like to get them back."

I shook my head. "There weren't any other photo albums or scrap books in there."

"Where's the box? Could we take a look?" Carson asked.

I frowned toward my car. "Well, I guess so..."

"Great!" Carson took off toward the car and Derek and I followed.

I opened the back hatch and the empty cargo bay reminded me that I'd been in such a hurry to rush out while Pandora was occupied with the catnip that I'd left the box at home. "Oh, sorry guys ... I left the box at home."

"That's okay. We don't need those old books." Derek's eyes darkened as he looked up at the mansion. "We have enough stuff in there. The photo album is one thing, but forget about all those old dusty books."

Derek steered Carson back toward the garage and I remembered I wanted to talk to Idris about the bronzes.

"Hey, I was wondering if I could ask your grandfather about those bronzes," I said. "I knocked on the door but no one answered."

Derek scowled up at the house. "Grandfather is very ill. We're not entertaining visitors in the house."

"Oh, okay." I felt disappointed about the bronzes, but maybe I could find out more about Felicity. "Maybe your mother remembers?"

"Mother?" No, I doubt it. She doesn't take much of an interest in that stuff." Derek reached into his pocket. "Thanks for bringing by the photo album. What do I owe you?"

I flapped my hand in the air. "Forget about it. I couldn't sell it to anyone else, anyway."

"Great. Then thanks for stopping by." Derek turned around, dismissing me, and I watched the two of them walk back to the garage.

I had no choice but to get in my car and drive away, disappointment following me like a black cloud.

As the stone mansion grew smaller in my rear view mirror, I got the funny feeling that there was something strange about the Bates family, and it wasn't just because their house looked like it should be in a horror movie.

Chapter Twenty-Four

I took a detour on my way back to the bookstore. I wanted to get the box of books I'd left at home so I'd have some new stock for the store.

Pulling into the driveway, I trotted up the farmer's porch steps and opened the door, expecting to be greeted by an angry Pandora.

The box sat on the kitchen table, right where I'd left it. I hefted it up against my hip, noticing the odd silence in the house.

"Pandora?"

Silence.

She must be really mad. I pictured her silently glaring at me from the living room sofa, or maybe hacking up a hairball on my bed.

I peeked into the living room. No cat, just the sun glinting off the paperweight, which reflected the books from my bookshelf on its curved surface.

Putting down the box, I went over to get the one thing that would bring her running—a can of cat food.

I popped open the top. Usually, the sound would entice her from even the most remote part of the house, but this time she didn't come.

I made a lot of noise putting the food into a bowl, but still no Pandora. Glancing over at the cat door, I realized she must have gone out.

"Well, I'm sure she can take care of herself," I said to no one as I picked the box back up and headed for my Jeep.

The books shifted in the box on the seat beside me as I drove to the bookstore. I probably *should* let Derek and Carson look through them before I stocked them on my shelves. I knew there were no more photo albums or scrapbooks, but some of the books were ancient and if they'd had a book in a collection, it should probably go back to the family.

I didn't have time to go back there now, though. I wanted to open the shop for the full afternoon and hopefully make up for all the time I'd been taking off.

I parked in my spot behind the shop and dragged the box inside, setting it down behind the counter. Potential customers were already peering in the windows, so I hurried over to unlock the door and turn the sign to 'Open'.

Customers filed in immediately and I enjoyed a busy afternoon with almost record sales. Unfortunately, I didn't have any time to look at the books in the box or call the Bates'. I'd been so busy, I didn't even notice it was past five p.m. when the steady stream of customers died down.

The approaching dinner hour emptied the streets and I closed up shop, taking the chance to sneak away and visit Emma over at the church. I doubted she was the one that killed Lavinia, but she did mention she needed money and she *was* hiding something. If nothing else, maybe I could find out what secret Lavinia and Ophelia shared.

***

The white doors of the church loomed in front of me. They were big, standing about twelve-feet tall. And they were locked.

Oversized brass latches adorned the front. I pulled and tugged on them, but the doors wouldn't open. Did the church close? I thought it was always open.

I turned away from the doors, my shoulders slumping. I was batting zero in my investigation today—I hadn't been able find out anything about the bronzes and now I wouldn't be able to talk to Emma, either.

"Mew."

I turned to my left and recognized the ginger-colored cat Pandora had had the altercation with behind the library. Come to think of it, I'd seen the same cat at Lavinia's funeral.

I crouched down and put my hand out.

"Here, Kitty," I crooned, trying to lure the cat over.

The cat looked at me with disdain, then turned toward the woods, walked a few steps, then turned back to look at me again.

"Meow."

The cat swung around and headed toward the woods again, pausing a second to look back over its shoulder at me, almost as if it was trying to get me to follow it.

Should I?

I hesitated on the church steps, trying to remember what was in that direction. I knew the church owned a lot of land in addition to the piece I was standing on where the church was built and the large parcel behind it where the cemetery was. The wooded area the cat was heading into was also part of the church property, but hadn't been developed yet.

The cat was at the edge of the woods now, looking back at me.

"What the heck," I said out loud, and started into the woods after it.

The dense woods blocked out most of the late afternoon sun and a damp chill settled on me as I followed the cat. Surprisingly, my leg didn't hurt. I hoped it was finally getting better.

The cat was following a path and we hadn't walked far when a rustling sound to my right caused my heart to jerk. I whipped my head toward it. Just another cat. I breathed a sigh of relief as I recognized the gray tiger cat as one that had been behind the library when I'd found the embosser.

I kept following the orange cat while the gray tiger kept pace over to my right, but at a safe distance. Just when I was starting to wonder if I'd made a mistake, an unkempt building appeared. It looked like some sort of storage building—large, with a door on the front but only one window on the side.

We were about ten feet away when the door opened slowly. My breath caught in my throat as Emma backed out of the building.

Emma whirled around, leaving the door open behind her.

"What are *you* doing here? This is church property!" Her voice rose in a pitch of anger ... and maybe even a little anxiety.

Stainless steel bowls clanked together in her hands and I leaned sideways to see into the building behind her.

She stood her ground, legs firmly planted as if she was guarding Fort Knox. What was in there? A stash of crucifixes? Frankincense and Myrrh? What could possibly be so important in a church storage shed ... and what was with those bowls?

Elspeth appeared in the doorway and I sucked in another surprised breath.

"Elspeth?" My brows mashed together as I stared at my neighbor. What was *she* doing here?

"It's okay, Emma," Elspeth said sweetly. "Willa is a friend."

Emma eyed me dubiously as she stepped aside.

"Not many people know about this place." Elspeth held out her arm, beckoning me closer. "We try to keep it secret, because there are some that would do us harm. Your grandma was a big supporter, though."

"Supporter?" Apparently, I'd been reduced to one-word questions.

"Yes," Elspeth's radiant smile lit her face as she stepped aside. "Come on in and I'll show you."

***

The windows on either end let filtered light into the dim interior. It took a few seconds for my eyes to adjust. When they did, I stared in wonder.

"Cats?" I raised my brows at Elspeth.

The building must have been about sixteen by twenty feet. The entire perimeter was stacked with wooden platforms loaded with straw. Bales of hay were strewn about. An occasional wooden kindling box lay on the floor. A row of stainless steel bowls holding cat food and water lined the far end.

Cats lounged around the perimeter. Several of them ran off as I entered. Others remained lounging, peering at me warily, coiled to spring up and run if I came too close. A few ignored me altogether. I recognized a couple of them from the day behind the library.

"These are feral cats," Elspeth said. "As you can see, we have quite a few that we try to keep warm and fed."

I crouched down, trying to coax one over.

"Most of them won't go near humans." Emma crouched down beside me, apparently warming to me now that she knew I had Elspeth's stamp of approval. She stuck out her hand and clucked.

A ball of black and white fur darted out from behind a bale of hay. It was the small black and white kitten with the tattered ear. She came over to Emma and licked her hand, then eyed me tentatively. I held my hand still and she ventured over, letting me pet her behind the ear.

"The friendly ones like her," Emma nodded toward the kitten as she scampered back behind the hay bale, "we try to adopt out to a good home. The others are too wild to adopt, so we provide shelter and food for them here."

Now I knew where Elspeth had acquired her growing collection of cats.

"Why in here?" I asked.

Elspeth and Emma looked at each other. Elspeth's face grew sad.

"Unfortunately, there are some who would harm our cause," Emma said.

"Really? Why?" Being an animal lover myself, I couldn't imagine who would oppose feeding starving animals.

"Some people in this town think the feral cats are dirty and will drive away the tourists that come to spend money," Emma said.

"So we hide back here." Elspeth looked around the room. "We've had to move the operation to different buildings three times in the past few years."

"And there's been some from the 'opposition' that come sneaking around the church trying to find the location. That's why I might have seemed a bit unfriendly to you in the church the other day." Emma looked at her feet.

"That's understandable," I said. I remembered the jingly object she'd been hiding behind her back. It had been a cat toy! That day, Emma had also said Lavinia donated to our causes. "Did Lavinia know about the cats?"

Emma glanced at Elspeth who nodded.

"Yes, she came twice a week to feed them and helped us out financially. In fact, she was here the morning she died," Emma said.

That explained why Lavinia lied about the candles—she was protecting the cats. Did that also explain why Ophelia lied?

"Would Ophelia Withington be one of the opposers?" I asked.

The look on Emma's face gave it away. "That woman! I hate to speak ill of anyone, but she was one of the worst ones. Once Pete died, it became an obsession with her. Pastor Foley discovered her skulking around the church ... she isn't a member, so I assume she was trying to figure out where we sheltered the cats. She said they got into some of the empty houses she was trying to sell and brought down property values—she wanted them all to be euthanized!"

My heart twisted as I looked at the cats. No wonder I didn't like her. Sure, she had seemed nicer since she'd been a victim of one of Pepper's teas, but who knew how long that would last? Besides, anyone who wanted to euthanize animals just because they brought down property values was no one to be friends with in my book. I found myself wishing, once again, that Ophelia was the killer.

Ophelia had been in town that morning, trying to find the cats. She'd provided an airtight alibi for the time of Lavinia's murder, but what if Emma had seen someone else in town that morning? She was out and about early enough and it was worth asking.

"Emma, was there anyone else around that morning ... the morning Lavinia died? Maybe someone else who was trying to uncover the cat shelter?"

Emma pressed her lips together. "The Bates family is another one of our opposers. At least, most of them are. I've seen that woman sniffing around in the woods trying to find the shelter, but not that morning. *That* morning I saw her son in that chauffeured car they come around in sometimes."

"Which son? Derek?" I'd known both Derek and Carson since we were little kids and found it hard to believe either of them would be cat-haters.

"I think so. Yes, it was Derek. I saw him sneaking around here early in the morning around six. I avoided detection by hiding behind a tree," Emma said proudly. "It was weird, though, because later on ... about seven ... I was all done with the cats and getting coffee at the cafe when I saw someone run out of the woods on the other side of the street—about a hundred feet up from the library—and jump into that fancy chauffeured car the Bates' have. It must have been him, but I have no idea what he would have been doing all that time."

"Maybe scouring the woods on both sides for the shelter?" Elspeth offered.

Emma shrugged. "Maybe. I'm just glad he didn't find it."

"But that would be a good sign. If he had to look on both sides, it means they don't really know where the shelter is now," Elspeth said.

"But you're sure you saw him?" I asked.

"Oh, yes. I wasn't that far from him in the woods, and who could miss that big old car they have?"

The car must have been the same one Ophelia had seen. I'd seen the car myself earlier that day in the garage. There was no question … Derek had been in town at the time of Lavinia's murder. Should I add him to the suspect list? The only problem was, I wasn't sure if he met any of the other criteria. His family was rich as anything, so he certainly didn't need money.

I thought back to earlier in the day … had he been wearing a ring? No, I was sure he hadn't been. Since Lavinia had mentioned it, I'd programmed myself to look at everyone's hands and I was sure I would have noticed.

But the truth was, he had been speeding away from town that morning. The only question was … had he been speeding away in frustration because he couldn't find the cat shelter, or had he been fleeing because he'd just committed murder?

Chapter Twenty-Five

Pandora woke from a long sleep, stretching her legs out lazily. She slitted one eye open. Where was she? Rolling on her back, the soft blanket underneath cushioned her while she watched a rectangle of light play on the plywood floor.

Opening both eyes, she remembered chasing the mouse up into the attic where she'd promptly fallen asleep on the old blanket. The blanket had been Anna's and she often came up here to feel closer to her previous human. It comforted her.

But now it was time to get up—she knew she'd been asleep for a long time. Catnip always made her so tired. And hungry.

She rolled onto all fours, pushed her front paws out in a stretch that elongated her back, then shook and trotted downstairs.

The smell of savory salmon feast tweaked her nose as she approached the stairs. Had Willa come home? Her heightened senses told her the house was empty now, but she did vaguely remember hearing Willa call for her while she was sleeping.

In the kitchen, she had her answer. Willa had been here and conveniently filled her cat dish. It looked like her training of the human was beginning to pay off.

Sticking her tongue out tentatively, she licked the top of the food. It was a little dry indicating it must have been sitting out for a while. Normally, Pandora would turn her nose up at such an insulting meal, but she was unusually ravenous, so she dug in to the mound with gusto.

A glow in the living room caught her attention. It was that thing again—the globe on the coffee table that was apt to glimmer at odd times. She tried to ignore it—thinking it quite impertinent that it thought it could summon her so easily.

Her eyes kept sliding over to the living room as she ate. So once she was done, she licked her paws, washed her face and then made her way over to see what the thing wanted.

Pandora slinked over to the coffee table, approaching it from the side, her gaze intent on the orb. It sparked with color, drawing her closer. She stood on her hind legs, reaching her front paw out tentatively to bat at the sphere.

Now that she was eye level, she could see what she thought were things moving inside. Movement like that was something no cat could resist and she leapt onto the coffee table—something Willa would not approve of—to get a better look.

She looked down into the orb, her eyes growing large, the pupils turning to thin slits as she stared inside.

There was something in here ... it looked like the inside of Elspeth's barn. Pandora could see the other cats gathered around. They looked up at her from inside the ball and she had an irresistible urge to go join them at the barn ... she knew something was very wrong.

***

It took only a few minutes for Pandora to run through the woods to the barn. The other cats were inside, just as she'd seen in the paperweight.

"What took you so long?" Otis admonished.

"I was sleeping." Pandora sat down and flicked her tongue over her back, washing herself as if she hadn't a care in the world. "Did you want something?"

"Things are coming to a head and we must keep the evil ones from getting what they seek." Inkspot's baritone rumbled from atop a hay bale.

Pandora wondered why he had to always be so vague. What evil ones and what were they seeking? "And...?"

Pandora didn't like the way the other cats were all looking at each other, as if they knew something she didn't and were afraid to tell her.

Snowball trotted over and sat beside her. "We think your human may be in danger."

Pandora's stomach twisted. "What do you mean?"

"Willa has the key ... they will try to take it from her," Truffles purred.

"What key?" Pandora wracked her memory ... had she seen Willa with a key?

"That's not important now. They're coming for it and we must come up with a plan to protect her," Otis cut in.

Pandora shot to her feet. Willa was in trouble and she had to help her. "What do you mean? Where?"

"I've got intel that leads me to believe they are going to Willa's house tonight," Tigger spoke up from the back of the barn.

Tonight! Panic clutched Pandora's heart. She had to get home and save Willa!

"Thanks!" Pandora turned and sped toward the barn door.

"Wait! We must form a proper plan!" Inkspot yelled after her.

"There's no time!" Pandora shot back.

"Impetuous fool will get herself killed." She heard Otis's disapproving tone as she shot into the woods.

Ignoring his words, she raced toward home as fast as she could, stopping only long enough to *sharpen her shivs on the bark of a tree—she had a feeling she might need them to be razor sharp tonight. Her feline instincts were on high alert. Trouble was coming and she'd have to do whatever she could to stop it.*

Chapter Twenty-Six

After talking to Emma and Elspeth, I stopped in at *The Mystic Cafe* for supper. I wasn't up for another English muffin jalapeño pizza and I didn't have anything else at home. Pandora would be mad, but I'd left the food out for her at noontime, so at least she wouldn't go hungry.

I sat by the window, watching the sunset and eating an Italian sub. If what Emma had said was true, I should add Derek to my suspect list. He was in town at that time, so he had opportunity ... but did he have motive?

So far, I had been operating on the theory that the killer was after the bronzes for financial gain, but what if there was another motive? I wondered if the police had come up with anything else, which made my thoughts turn to Striker.

I hadn't seen him since I threw up on his shoes and I wondered if he had been avoiding me. Chances were he probably never wanted to see me again.

"Easy come, easy go," I muttered to myself as I tossed out my sandwich wrappings and headed to my Jeep.

It was dark by the time I pulled into my driveway. The pitch-black moonless night enveloped my car as soon as I shut the headlights off. Ever since I'd reached my mid-forties, my eyes had been taking longer and longer to adjust to the darkness and tonight was no different.

Which was why I didn't notice anything wrong with my door until it swung open on its own when I tried to insert the key.

***

I stared into the dark interior of my house, adrenalin shooting through my veins.

Was someone in there?

I strained to hear even the slightest noise, but the house was silent. Grabbing the baseball bat I kept next to the door, I inched my way in, flicking the light switch, then immediately lifting the bat behind my head, ready to swing at anything that came at me.

The house was empty. Or at least the kitchen was.

I'd left in a hurry. Maybe I hadn't closed the door fully?

I crept further into the kitchen where I could see into the living room and the heart-thudding scene turned my legs to jelly and answered my question.

The living room was a mess!

My large floor-to-ceiling bookcase had been pulled away from the wall and rested on its back on the floor. Books lay strewn in piles around it, their formerly pristine pages torn and creased. The cushions had been tossed from the sofa and chairs and lay about the room.

My heart thudded against my ribcage as I ran back to the porch, my fingers tapping Augusta's number on my cell phone.

Even though I was sure no one was still in the house, I sat on the porch and waited for Augusta to arrive. It didn't take long and within ten minutes, I was back in the living room with her, my stomach sinking at the sight of my ruined book collection.

"Did they take anything?" Augusta frowned at the overturned bookshelf.

I studied the pile, the feeling of being violated blooming in my gut. "Impossible to tell."

"What about the rest of the house?"

"I haven't looked. I saw the mess in here and called you right away."

"Okay, let me check it out." Augusta headed toward the stairs, peeking first into the dining room on the other side, and then headed up.

I was about to follow her when another car pulled into my driveway.

Striker.

He jumped out of the car, bounding into the kitchen. My stomach lurched and I wondered if he was thinking about the last time he saw me—when I threw up on his shoes.

He didn't seem to be holding that against me now. He rushed to my side and it seemed like he was going to hug me until he stopped short, just inches away. Probably trying to keep his shoes at a safe distance.

"Chance, are you okay?" My heart warmed at the concern in his eyes.

I ran my hands through my curls. "Yeah, I'm fine. I came home and found my living room in shambles."

"Let's see." He led the way into the house and we entered the living room just as Augusta was coming down the stairs.

Striker eyed the mess. "Is that the extent of the damage?"

"I think so," Augusta answered. "Nothing out of place upstairs or in the dining room or kitchen."

"I don't understand," I said. "What would someone want in here? I don't have anything valuable or important. Do you think this has something to do with Lavinia's murder?"

Striker and Augusta exchanged a glance. Did they know something I didn't?

Striker shrugged. "You never know."

"But I didn't have any bronzes or anything on the shelf. Just books."

"Were any of them valuable ... or did you have any of those hollowed-out books that you can hide stuff in?" Augusta asked.

I shook my head.

"What about papers inside the books?" Striker asked.

"No, nothing." My stomach sank as I bent down to pick up one of the books. Glancing at the pile, I could see most of them were ruined. They weren't valuable, but I had kept them in pristine condition and now, with the pages folded and the spines stretched, they would never be worth anything.

But it wasn't just about the value of the books. I loved books and seeing them treated with such disrespect grated on me.

I placed the book back on the pile and it seemed to sigh in disappointment.

"Did you hear that?" Augusta frowned at the pile.

"What?" I cocked my ear toward it and that's when I heard it.

The faintest, most pitiful meow I'd ever heard.

"Pandora!" I dug at the pile furiously. I'd assumed she'd run off when whoever broke in had ransacked the house. Had she been lying underneath the books, hurt the whole time?

My heart twisted as I uncovered a lump of gray fur.

Pandora lay on her side. The end of her tail bent at an impossible angle. Blood matted the fur on the side of her head. I reached out to touch her and she stirred slightly, then sighed and lay still.

Tears burned my eyes as I gently freed her from the pile.

Striker had knelt beside me and he reached out, touching her neck.

"She's alive!" He turned to Augusta. "Call Doc Evans, he'll open the animal hospital up for me."

Striker gently took Pandora from my arms and we ran for his car.

***

My heart crowded my throat and tears burned my eyes as I stared at Pandora's still form on the stainless steel exam table. Her shaved arm stuck out straight to the side, IV lines running from the needles that pinched her tender skin in several places. The side of her head had also been shaved, the long gash closed with ugly stitches.

"She took a beating. Put up a good fight, too," Doc Evans said. "But she'll be fine. Just needs some rest."

I nodded, unable to speak.

"She's in good hands." Striker put his arm around me and I nodded again, my eyes riveted on the still form of my cat.

I knew she was in good hands. Doc Evans was a pediatrician who had retired to become a veterinarian. He'd been a great pediatrician, but was even better with pets. Some said he had a calling for it. If anyone could mend Pandora, it was Doc Evans.

"You should get some rest, too. But I don't think you should go home alone," Striker said, turning me gently toward the door. "I called Pepper to come and get you. She said you could stay at her place."

"You did?" I croaked the words out, my throat raw with emotion. I felt a stab of jealousy—when did Striker get Pepper's number and how often had he been calling her?

"Yes. She said she'd be here any minute." Striker looked through the window of the examination room to the dark, empty reception area then back at me. "Will you be okay until then? I want to go back to your house and help Augusta inspect the crime scene."

"Sure." I opened the door and he followed me out into the lobby. Since it was after-hours, there was no receptionist, no customers waiting, which suited me just fine. I could use some alone time.

We stood looking at each other awkwardly. I wondered what Striker was thinking ... and why my stomach was flip-flopping.

Then the door opened and Elspeth swept in, breaking the spell.

"Where is she?" Elspeth's worried eyes darted between the three examining room doors.

"In here." I started toward the room Pandora was in. Striker gave me a wave and moved toward the door to the parking lot.

"Thanks," I called after him. He turned and nodded to me, then was gone.

Elspeth was already at Pandora's side, her hands lovingly caressing the cat's fur.

"What happened?" She looked at me with puckered brows.

"Someone broke into my house and ransacked my living room. Pandora must have been there. I found her like this, under a pile of books."

"Books?"

I nodded.

Elspeth's face hardened and she pressed her forehead against Pandora's, all the while crooning softly to the cat.

Pandora's tail lifted a fraction of an inch, the kinked end sticking straight up in the air. Her eyelids fluttered, then opened. She gazed into Elspeth's eyes as if the two of them were having some sort of telepathic communication.

Pandora put her paw on Elspeth's forearm and Elspeth nodded, then turned the paw gently in her hand. Pandora's claws shot out, revealing broken jagged edges.

"She fought the intruder," Elspeth squeezed her paw gently and I saw the pinkie claw pop out. My breath caught in my throat ... skewered on the claw was a scrap of navy blue fabric.

"That looks like the same fabric that was on the murder weapon. I should get Augusta to look at that." I pulled the fabric off, found a plastic baggie on one of the drawers, and deposited it inside.

Holding the bag up in front of me, I felt a spark of hope. "I don't know why the person who killed Lavinia would break into my house, but maybe this scrap of fabric will help the police figure things out."

"That's not the only thing that might help them," Elspeth said.

"What do you mean?"

"Judging by Pandora's claws, she fought hard. Your intruder couldn't have escaped being marked. Find the person with claw marks on their arm, and you may have found your killer."

Chapter Twenty-Seven

"You think the person who broke into your house was the same person who killed Lavinia?" Pepper's brow creased as she tucked the soft, mint-colored chenille blanket around my legs.

"Well, the color looked the same and it is a strange coincidence."

I'd called Augusta from the animal hospital and she'd come right away to pick up the navy blue piece of fabric. According to her, they hadn't found any clues to go on at my house. Striker had insisted on righting my bookshelf and putting the books back, which somehow made me feel all warm and fuzzy. Or maybe the warm and fuzzy feeling came from the tea Pepper was pumping into me as I sat tucked into an overstuffed chair, safe and warm inside her country cottage.

"But what's the connection?" She poured more tea into my cup.

"I have no idea, but now I'm starting to think the murder didn't have anything to do with the bronzes, and I got the impression Augusta and Striker might think so, too."

"Well, if it wasn't about the bronzes, then what?"

I shook my head and took a sip of tea. I don't know what Pepper had put in it, but it sure was relaxing me.

"Maybe if we look at the suspects, it will make more sense," Pepper said.

"Oh, that reminds me, I do have a new suspect since I last talked to you." I told her about my conversation with Emma.

"Derek Bates? But he always seems so nice." Pepper screwed her face up. "I can't picture him being a killer."

"True, but I can't picture Bing or Josiah being the killer either."

"I hate to think it's any of them. Can't you come up with someone else?"

"I've tried and, other than Ophelia, who has an alibi, those three are the only ones who had means, motive or opportunity."

"But, which one of them had all three?"

"That's a good question." I chewed on my bottom lip while I thought about it. "All three of them were in town that morning, so they all had opportunity."

"And any one of them had the means to clobber Lavinia and push her ... you don't have to be too strong to do that."

"So, that leaves motive." I put my teacup down and snuggled into the chair. "And if the killer wasn't after the bronzes, we're not really sure *what* the motive is."

"It could still be financial," Pepper said. "You said they ransacked your bookcase. Maybe they were after a valuable book?"

"But, I don't have a valuable book."

"Not that you *know* of, but have you checked all those books lately? Maybe one became rare for some reason ... the author died or whatever. Or maybe you just never knew you had a rare one."

"Maybe." I did a mental inventory of my books. Some had been my grandmother's. I thought I knew the inventory pretty well, but maybe I'd missed a rare one.

"So who needed money?" Pepper asked.

"Not Bing or Derek ... maybe Josiah. He can't make much on the postmaster's pension."

"Josiah could probably use some extra money, but Derek's not rich, either." Pepper took my teacup and walked around the center chimney to the kitchen area. "Idris controls the Bates fortune and he doesn't hand money out easily, so Derek doesn't really have any of his own."

I stifled a yawn. "So it's between Josiah and Derek."

"Not necessarily." Pepper took a pillow out of the hall closet and started making up the sofa for me to sleep on, which was a good thing since my eyelids felt like someone had tied lead weights to them. "You can't forget about the clues. The navy blue cape, the ring and the gray hair."

"Josiah doesn't wear a ring. I have no idea if Derek or Josiah have a blue cape, but I know Bing does—his magician's cape. *And* he has gray hair and a ring."

Pepper screwed her face up. "I'm trying to think, but I remember Derek has dark hair. So, only Bing and Josiah have gray hair."

"This is confusing. It could be any of them." I moved over to the sofa, nestling under the soft covers.

"Or anyone else." Pepper tucked the blanket under the sofa cushion and pecked my cheek. "But it's late and you must be exhausted. Let's get some sleep and we can think more about it in the morning.

"Mmmhmm." I mumbled my response, almost fully asleep.

As I drifted off, my subconscious mind sifted through the clues and suspects. Visions of rings, capes and murder weapons passed before my closed eyelids. The pieces snapped into place just before I fell into the deep abyss of sound sleep.

Suddenly, I knew who matched all three clues ... and I had a good idea how to prove he was the killer.

Chapter Twenty-Eight

I leaned on the counter at my bookstore, tapping my finger impatiently on its polished wood surface. I'd come in early, after checking on Pandora, and set the wheels in motion.

Today, Lavinia's killer would be brought to justice.

Outside, dark clouds had settled over the mountain. The smell of rain permeated my senses and the humidity frizzed my hair and made my leg ache. I bent down to massage it, jerking my head up as the bells over the door tinkled.

"Morning Willa." Hattie and Cordelia, in matching purple raincoats sauntered in. Cordelia had an extra Styrofoam cup, which she handed to me.

"Thanks." I tipped the cup toward her, then took a sip.

The door opened again and in came Bing, followed by Josiah. I noticed they both wore trench coats, but that wasn't unusual given the rainy forecast. Josiah shrugged his off and took a seat on the couch, rolling his sleeves up. His arms were not marred with scratches, which supported my theory.

Josiah was not the killer.

Bing sat on the couch next to him. He didn't remove his raincoat. I glanced nervously at the big ring on his hand.

"I heard about the break-in at your place." Bing turned concerned eyes on me. "Are you okay?"

"News travels fast. I'm fine."

"And Pandora?" My heart warmed at the genuine concern in Hattie's voice.

"She'll be fine," I said. "Doc Evans is just watching her for another night."

"Oh, good," Hattie and Cordelia said in unison.

The door opened again and the four gray heads swiveled to see Augusta enter, her brows raised in question.

"Hi, everyone," Augusta turned to me. "I got your cryptic message. What's this about?"

I took a deep breath. "I think I know who Lavinia's killer is, and I'm going to prove it right now."

Augusta raised her brows.

Hattie and Cordelia gasped.

Bing frowned, his bushy white brows practically covering his eyes. "Now, Willa ...."

Josiah cocked his head, rubbing his chin. "You don't say."

Out of the corner of my eye, I saw a wispy swirl starting to form at the end of the cookbook aisle. Figures, Lavinia would show up now when I didn't need her.

I turned away from Lavinia's ghost in time to see Augusta roll her eyes at me.

"Willa, how many times do I have to tell you not to investigate on your own? If you have a theory about the killer, you should tell me and let the police do the proper investigation."

The door jingled open, saving me from having to answer, and everyone turned to see Derek Bates step inside the shop.

Lavinia's ghost was doing her best to distract me. I could see her out of the corner of my eye down at the other end of the store where she was gesturing and gyrating. You'd think she'd be happy I was getting ready to unmask her killer, but instead she looked concerned. I turned my back on her.

"Hi, everyone." Derek scanned the group uncertainly before resting his gaze on me. "Willa, you said you have a book for me."

"Hi Derek." I avoided his question. "I think you know everyone here."

"Umm ... yeah." He made a face and pushed a lock of hair back from his forehead, revealing the gray streak. "What's going on? Where's the book?"

"There isn't any book," I said.

"What?" What are you talking about?"

Derek was still standing by the door and I was on the other side of couches. Everyone's heads were swiveling back and forth between Derek and me like they were watching a tennis match.

I decided to move in for the kill.

"Emma at the church told me she saw you skulking around here the morning Lavinia Babbage was killed."

Derek scrunched his face up. "What? When was that? ... Oh. Yes, I remember now. I *was* in town ... but surely you don't think I had anything to do with *that*?"

I looked down at his hand. Where was his ring?

Lavinia had made her way over to the counter and was gesturing at me again. I turned to the side, ignoring her.

Doubt started to bloom in my gut—maybe Derek wasn't the killer. But he *had* to be—the clues all led to him.

He was young and strong, with the means to clobber and push an old lady.

He was seen in the area at the time of death.

He needed money and knew about the bronzes in the library... if the bronzes were even still the motive.

Even though his hair was dark, he did have that streak of gray. Lavinia could have easily reached back and grabbed on to that exact spot of hair.

And, even though he wasn't wearing a ring now, I'd remembered what had niggled at me about the photo of him with his brother, father and grandfather holding the family crest in the photo album—they'd all been wearing matching family crest rings.

Not only that, but I'd seen a long black car in the Bates' garage—just like the one Ophelia described fleeing town that morning. And hanging next to that were dark driver's coats. Sure, I hadn't been able to make out the color in the dark, but I was willing to bet they were navy blue.

He could deny it all he wanted—the real killer usually did.

I noticed everyone was staring at me so I continued. "Isn't it true that you're in need of money? You don't have much of your own and your grandfather controls the family money."

Derek's face pinched and he shuffled his feet. "Well, yes, but I don't see what—"

"And you knew about the valuable bronzes in the library," I cut him off.

"The ones grandfather donated? That you keep pestering us about?"

Lavinia was practically doing cartwheels on the counter. I ignored her—I was almost finished, and then we'd have this whole thing behind us and Lavinia could go off to wherever ghosts went off to.

I narrowed my eyes at Derek. "Where were you last night around six p.m.?"

"Huh? I was home ... just what is going on here?"

"My house was broken into by Lavinia's killer and I think you know *exactly* what is going on because you had means, motive and opportunity." I ticked the last three words off on my fingers.

"That's crazy!" The words exploded from Derek's mouth. "I didn't kill Lavinia or break into your house!"

"Really? Then explain why you were skulking around in the woods just before the murder and were seen fleeing town right after in your long black car."

A confused look passed over Derek's face. "Long black car? You mean the Lincoln? I never take that car ... and if you must know, I was bringing my cat to the vet that morning."

I remembered what Emma had said about Derek being one of the 'opposers' of the feral cat sanctuary. "Cat? I heard you didn't even like cats, so now I know you're lying."

"That's not true," Derek said. "The rest of my family doesn't like them, which is why I had to take Kitty to Doc Evans early in the morning. I keep him in my wing of the house ... away from the others. Anyway, he jumped out of the window of my Mini-Cooper on the way through town and ran into the woods. I was in there trying to catch him."

What? If that was true, it blew my whole case. The back of my mind wondered if Doc Evans could give him an alibi, but my mouth couldn't be stopped. "I think you're lying—covering up. That's what killers do."

"Willa—" Augusta tried to cut in.

"No. Wait." I held my hand up to Augusta. "I can prove it."

I took two long strides to Derek's side, grabbed his sleeve and pushed it up to the elbow, turning triumphant eyes to Augusta. "See!"

Augusta squinted at Derek's arm. "See what?"

I whipped my head back to look at his arm, my stomach sinking. There were no scratches. I pushed up the other sleeve only to find that arm was scratch free, too.

"But that's impossible," I said. "Pandora fought the intruder and Elspeth said they would have scratches on their forearm!"

Derek jerked his arms away. "Well, I'm not the one who broke in, which is why I don't have any scratches. And I certainly am not the one who killed Lavinia Babbage!"

And with that, Derek stormed out the door, leaving an embarrassing silence in his wake.

I looked around the room, my leaden stomach growing even heavier. Everyone was staring at me, even Lavinia, who stood behind the counter, hands on hips.

Josiah cleared his throat and pushed up from the couch. "Well, I should be going."

"Yep," Bing said.

"Us, too," Cordelia and Hattie twittered as the four of them fought their way to be first out the door.

Augusta gave me a look of disappointment, then wordlessly shook her head and disappeared out the door behind the others.

"Sorry..." I mumbled, staring at the closed door.

Had I accused Derek wrongly? It certainly seemed like I had. I'd wanted to reveal the killer and help Augusta out, but I'd only made a fool of myself and made Augusta mad. She'd probably never trust my instincts again.

And the worst part was that if neither Derek nor Josiah were the killer, that left only one person on my suspect list ... Bing.

Chapter Twenty-Nine

I looked around the empty bookstore. Apparently, even Lavinia was disappointed in me —she was nowhere to be seen.

Slipping behind the counter, I lowered myself to the stool, my shoulders slumping in defeat. Glancing down, I saw the box of books I'd put there yesterday.

Nothing like looking at old books to pick up one's spirits.

I rummaged in the box, picking out a thick book bound in soft brown leather. It was heavy— about four hundred pages, the edges dipped in gold leaf, almost completely worn off with centuries of use.

How many centuries? Certain that it was at least one hundred years old, I opened it up to search for a date.

It was a strange book. No publishing information could be found. The pages were thicker than most old books. They rasped as I turned them, the smell of old paper wafting up to my nose.

It was handwritten in what looked like an old quill pen. But the words weren't English ... at least not most of them. I could barely make out what it said, but they were organized with a list at the top and then a few paragraphs at the bottom. Like a recipe book.

With a start, I realized this must be one of the Bates' ancestors hand written recipe books and probably of value to the family, especially considering the exquisite binding, which must have cost a fortune. I wondered if the recipes were any good.

I really should return it to the Bates', but I was too embarrassed to call Derek after what had just happened.

"Oh, I see you are finally getting a clue." Lavinia's ghost popped into view out of nowhere and I fumbled the book, almost sending it crashing to the floor, managing to save it at the last minute.

"Sorry, Lavinia," I said. "I really thought Derek was your killer."

"Why would Derek kill me?"

"For the money."

"Money? Haven't you figured out yet that this is about something far more important than money?

My brows mashed together. The truth was, I had been starting to think this had nothing to do with the bronzes. I just couldn't figure out what it *did* have to do with.

"You're holding the key right in your hand," Lavinia said as if reading my mind.

I looked down at the book which lay open in my lap. "This recipe book?"

"Those aren't recipes, Willa. That book holds something very important, and now you must protect it."

Her words made me uneasy. "Huh?"

"Sorry, I couldn't help you more earlier." Lavinia wrung her hands together. "The truth is, being a ghost isn't all it's cracked up to be. You aren't trusted with all the information up front. Anyway, I just now found out the real truth, which is why I was trying to get your attention when you were grilling Derek."

This was getting confusing. "So, you're saying this has nothing to do with the bronzes or money, but to do with this recipe book instead?"

"Not recipes, Willa," Lavinia bent down, her mouth close to my ear. "Spells."

"Spells?" I squinted at the book. "I guess spells could look like recipes. But that's ridiculous. Who would use these spells? Witches?"

Lavinia nodded solemnly.

"But, there's no such thing."

"Don't I wish it," Lavinia said. "Anyway, I cannot tell you how important this book is. There are forces of good and evil ... you don't want the evil forces to get a hold of it."

"But, how do I know who is good and who is evil?" I squinted up at her. I still wasn't even sure I believed the malarkey about spells and witches, but since I wasn't doing so well with my own theory, the least I could do was to hear her out.

"Oh, you'll know," she said.

"And you must be very, very careful," Robert Frost piped in from the purple couch where he was sitting with Franklin Pierce.

"Yes, Willa," Franklin added. "This is dangerous and important business and we don't want anything to happen to you."

Robert nodded. "We've gotten quite attached to you here in the bookshop. It just wouldn't be the same without you."

I was starting to feel like I was in a dream. Spells? Witches? Ghosts getting attached to me?

The three of them jerked their heads toward the door. Robert and Franklin swung back to look at me, their mouths forming round 'o's.

"Oh-oh," they said in unison before disappearing.

I turned to Lavinia who had a look of panic on her face. "Look out, Willa—my killer is coming. Remember, above all, you must protect the book!"

I looked back down at the book in my lap.

"I still don't understand what, exactly, is the big deal." I looked back up at Lavinia, but she was gone.

"Hey ..." I let my voice trail off. Leave it to a ghost to disappear with some vague warning and only half the answers I needed.

"Are you talking to someone?"

I whirled around at the sound of the voice, fingers of dread squeezing my heart when I saw who stood there ...

Bing Thorndike.

***

How did *he* get in? I hadn't heard the door jangle.

My eyes slid to his forearms, but he still had long sleeves, so I couldn't see the scratches Pandora had inflicted on him when he'd broken into my house. The break-in hadn't made sense last night, but now I knew the reason. I was holding it in my hands.

"Give me the book, Willa. I'll keep it safe." Bing reached out toward the book, the clunky gold Magician's Guild ring gleaming on his finger.

My mind whirled in confusion as Bing advanced on me, his face wore a smile that might have appeared friendly any other time, but looked menacing to me now.

I sat frozen on the stool. I couldn't give Bing the book—he was the killer! Handing the book over was the *last* thing I was going to do. Not just because I instinctively felt protective of the book, but I also feared he'd kill *me* once I handed it over.

Movement at the end of the inspirational books aisle caught my eye and I looked over to see Robert Frost pulling a book from the shelf.

Bang!

The sound of the book slamming to the floor distracted Bing and I ran toward the door.

"Willa! Wait! I'm trying to help you!" I heard Bing yell as I ran across the shop, the old book clutched to my chest.

My leg was burning, slowing me down. It seemed like I was running in chest-high water and my gut twisted as I realized it wasn't just because of my bum leg. Something strange was happening, as if time was slowing down.

I fought my way toward the door, a glance back over my shoulder showed Bing gaining ground. I closed my eyes, the sinking sensation in my chest overwhelming me ... I couldn't let Bing get me.

The memory of a book I once read surfaced. In the book, the hero could speed up time by turning the hands of their watch forward. *Too bad I don't wear a watch*, I thought, wishing with all my heart I had put one on that morning.

I looked down at my wrist. I *had* put one on! Not caring why I didn't necessarily remember putting it on that morning, I reached down and turned the small knob, the minute hand moving forward just as I felt Bing's heavy hand clutch my shoulder.

***

I was catapulted out the door onto the street, my face crushed into someone's chest.

I pulled away, the taste of wool in my mouth and my heart racing as I looked up into the surprised face of Carson Bates. His car sat idling behind him at the curb, the back door still open.

Relief flooded through me.

"Carson, thank goodness." I glanced behind me to see if Bing was catching up. "You gotta help me! We need to get out of here."

His eyes flew up and he stepped aside, gesturing toward the open door. I launched myself into the car and he slid in beside me, closing the door behind him.

"Go!" I yelled at the driver, who raised his brow at Carson in the rear view mirror. Carson nodded and the car shot forward.

I twisted in the seat, looking out the rear window, past the long length of the trunk to see Bing shoot out the door of my shop onto the street.

I pulled my cell phone out of my pocket. I needed to call Augusta, although I wasn't sure what I was going to say. Somehow I didn't think telling her Bing had slowed down time to take a recipe book from me was going to impress her.

"Not so fast," Carson said as I started to punch the numbers.

"Huh?" I looked over at him.

The phone turned molten hot in my hand and I dropped it with a squeal, pulling my hand back. As I watched it melt on the floor mat, I held my already blistering fingers against my chest.

I looked from the puddle of my phone to Carson, my brows mashed together. My brain felt a little slow on the uptake. My heart thudded against my ribcage.

What was going on?

"Thanks, Willa." Carson reached across the seat toward the book in my lap. A glimmer of gold on his finger caught my eye—the Bates family crest ring. "I was coming for this, but you saved me the trouble. How convenient."

I pulled the book away, instinctively trying to hide it behind my back on the other side of him. He stretched around me to grab the book, the sleeves of his navy blue coat pulled back, exposing his forearms.

My breath caught in my throat—his arms were raked with scratches.

Chapter Thirty

The hard, musty floor pressing on my shoulder blades alerted me to the fact that I was laying down. Dampness seeped through my sweatshirt. A dank, earthy smell tickled my nose. I opened one eye, the dim flicker of light from the single bulb in the ceiling seared into my eyeball with a stabbing pain.

Closing my eye, I rolled on my side, blinking my eyes open again as I fought the wave of nausea that rolled over me. Once it passed, I stared at my surroundings in disbelief.

I'd heard rumors that the Bates mansion had a real dungeon, but I didn't believe them. Until now. Now I *had* to believe it ... because I was in it.

The stone walls in the cavernous room were void of windows, the only source of light coming from the one dim bulb sticking out of the screw-in socket in the ceiling directly above me. It was clear the addition of electricity had been an afterthought down here in the basement.

To tell the truth, the depressing atmosphere would have been more appropriately illuminated by the ancient torches that sat unlit in their iron holders in the wall. Given the dim lighting, I could see only about twenty feet in front of me, after which the rest of the basement was shrouded in foreboding dark shadow.

Seeing twenty feet in front of me was enough, though. Enough to see that I was in some sort of iron cage, the bars going from floor to ceiling, the door held shut by an old iron lock. The cage was empty except for me and a thin layer of straw in the corner, which I hoped wasn't supposed to be my bed.

How did I get here?

I pushed myself up from the ground. The stinging pain in my hand as it touched the floor jolted my memory of the car ride with Carson.

My stomach twisted. It was Carson Bates who had broken into my house and likely him who killed Lavinia. He wore a big ring. He rode in the dark black car. He had the same gray streak in his hair as Derek.

And, when I'd run into him on the street, he was wearing one of the coats I'd seen in the Bates garage. A navy blue coat with oversized storm flaps on the shoulders and back. Those storm flaps could easily have been mistaken for a cape in the shadowy figure Lavinia had seen as she fell down the steps.

My head started to ache along with my hand and my leg as I tried to remember what had happened. The last thing I remembered was Carson trying to take the book from me in the car.

Seeing as how I didn't have the book now, he must have succeeded. Everything after that was a blank.

Did he knock me out, somehow? How had I gotten here? And where was I? I assumed it was the Bates' basement, but since I didn't remember getting here, I supposed it could be anywhere.

But what did it matter? No matter where I was, I needed to get out. Fast.

I walked over to the door and pushed. Naturally, it didn't budge—I couldn't be that lucky. I pulled on it with as much force as I could muster, but it was solid ... and locked tight.

I paced the perimeter of my ten by ten cell, studying the floor and ceiling to see if there were any cracks or openings I could wriggle out through. There were none. I tested every bar with my good hand until it stung from pulling on the chipped, rusty iron. None of them budged.

A sigh of frustration escaped my lips as I leaned against the wall. The hard, cold stones chilled my back as I sunk down to the floor.

My heart plummeted as I realized I was now trapped by the person who had killed Lavinia. I hugged my knees to my chest, put my head down and cried.

***

"Meow."

I lifted my head from the crook of my elbow, and brushed away hot tears. Did I just hear a cat? I thought about Pandora and my heart twisted.

Looking out at the edge of the darkness, I saw something slinking about. It *was* a cat. Not Pandora, though. This cat was white, with mocha colored markings.

"Here, Kitty," I put out my hand and made clucking noises.

The cat turned to face me, her pale blue eyes studying me intently as she crept closer.

She snaked her way throughout the bars and came to me, rubbing her cheek against my hand.

"Hi, there. Who are you?" I wondered. Was it Derek's cat? Now that I knew Carson was the killer, maybe Derek had been telling the truth. I wondered if Derek had been involved, too.

"Oh, well, what does it matter now?" I asked the cat as I found comfort in stroking the silky fur behind her ears.

As the cat's purring relaxed me, I worried what would happen to Pandora if I didn't make it out of there. I was glad she was safe at the animal hospital. If not for the break-in, she would have been at the bookstore with me and who knows what might have happened to her.

This brought my thoughts to what had happened in the store. It had all been about that old book. The book Lavinia had told me to protect.

I remembered how Bing had wanted the book, but I thought he was the enemy and ran from him. My stomach twisted ... I'd practically delivered the book right into Carson's hands, and now if something bad happened because of it, it was all on me.

I couldn't just sit here and let that happen. I had to do something.

I stood suddenly, causing the cat to let out a startled mew. I rushed to the door of my cell, the cat trotting in front of me, seeming to know where I was going before I even got there. I pressed my face against the bars, above the lock and looked down, trying to get a look at the lock opening.

The Bates mansion was over three hundred and fifty years old and the cell had probably been here for that long. The lock was original—a simple device that could be opened with a skeleton key. My years as a crime reporter had garnered me a lot of skills, not the least of which was basic lock picking.

I knew how to pick one of these. I just needed something long and straight. I searched my pockets, coming up empty.

"Damn!" My arms fell against my sides in frustration.

"Meow!" The cat had left the confines of the cage and was playing with what looked like a big dust ball. I watched as she batted it with her paw, sending it rolling and then pounced on it over and over again.

That gave me an idea.

Scanning the floor, I saw a long flat piece of metal that would make a perfect lock pick. It was too far for me to reach, but I might be able to use one of the tricks I'd learned from Bing to get the cat to do my work for me.

One of Bing's favorite tricks was to make things look like they floated in air. He used a fishing line for that, the line seeming invisible. I didn't have fishing line, but I had something Bing always said would work just as well—my hair.

The strands were thick, and the corkscrew curls made it look shorter than it actually was. I plucked a few strands out, pleased that I got two of the white ones, and tied them together. Then I picked a few pieces of straw from the corner and tied that to one end.

The dangling straw caught the cat's eye and she left her dust ball and trotted into the cell. Standing up on her hind legs, she batted at it.

"You like?" I squatted down and threw the straw end out. The cat skittered after it, pouncing on it. I jerked it out from under her and she skittered again.

I reeled in my new cat toy and went to the edge of the cell. Sticking my hand out through the bars, I tossed the toy out toward the metal piece. It landed just beyond it. Perfect.

The cat pounced on the toy, her front paw hitting the metal piece and sending it sliding toward the cell. Not far enough, though. I jerked the piece toward me and she hit the metal again, inching it closer. A few more well-placed tosses and the metal piece was within reach.

"Thanks, Kitty." I stretched my fingers through the bars, ignoring the throbbing pain of my burned fingertips, and grabbed the metal piece.

Standing, I poked my hand out so I could put the metal into the lock. The cat sat on the other side of the door, staring at me intently.

I dug the metal piece around. Turns out it's a lot harder picking a lock from the inside. After about five minutes of fiddling, I heard a satisfying click.

I pushed the door and it swung open.

Chapter Thirty-One

I stepped out of the cell, my heart thumping as my eyes darted around the room, or at least the part of the room I could see.

Which way should I go?

My senses told me I was in a basement because the air had that dank, damp underground feeling. But there were no windows like a regular basement.

My stomach tightened as I looked into the dark. I had no idea what I would find there, but there certainly wasn't any way out from where I was standing.

I forged ahead.

The cat stayed with me, following by my side. I had no idea what I was looking for, but maybe I could find a door that led outside. Or upstairs. Although, if I was in the Bates mansion as I suspected, going upstairs could be fatal.

"Mew." I heard the soft sound behind me and realized the cat had stopped. I turned, barely able to make her white form out in the dark. She was standing next to the wall ... no, not next to it—half-way inside it!

I bent down to find a crack in the wall. It was about five inches, big enough for the cat to wriggle through. She disappeared behind it, the reappeared a few seconds later.

"Meow!" She jerked her tail at me.

"Sure, I'd love to follow you, but it's too small. Guess I shouldn't have had dessert last night." I stuck my arm through and tried to wedge my shoulder in. It just wasn't big enough.

I pulled my arm out … or tried to. It was stuck.

"Meow." The cat weaved around my ankles.

"Yeah, thanks. This is just great." I jerked my arm and it came free, but not before I felt the stones shift slightly.

Was it my imagination … or had the opening widened?

I put my arm in again and this time more of my shoulder fit through. I wriggled and pushed. Pain shot through my bad leg as I used it for leverage, but it worked. The crack opened up enough for me to fit and I slid in.

I was in a narrow passageway. The cat flicked her tail impatiently before me as I stifled a sneeze from the dust tickling my nose. I could barely make out a set of stairs in front of me. At the top, thin slats of light that I assumed were coming from between the boards that made the passage allowed for minimum visibility.

Where was the light coming from?

The cat started up the steps and I followed.

We got to the top and there was an intersection. I peered through one of the lighted gaps into a large kitchen. It was empty, but the stainless steel appliances gleamed on top of black and white checked tile.

I limped a few more feet and peeked through another gap. This one revealed a sitting room decorated in pale blue. I realized I must have been in a secret passageway somewhere inside the house. All I needed to do was find a way out, hopefully in an unoccupied room with a door to the outside so I could make a clean get-away.

"Mew." The cat sat up ahead. Looking at me, then at the wall. At me, and then the wall. Clearly, she was trying to tell me something.

As I tiptoed up to her, I could hear voices. My blood chilled when I recognized one of them as Carson Bates.

The gap in the boards in front of the cat looked different from the others. It was a door. A secret doorway that led into the room. Pressing my face against one of the slats, I looked into an ornate library.

Bookshelves lined the walls. Two tufted leather sofas sat facing each other in the middle of the room. A large stone fireplace filled the opposite wall.

Idris Bates stood at the end of one of the sofas. Hadn't Derek said he was sick? He looked fine to me. Felicity sat on the sofa, her white, flowing dress spread out on the seat on either side of her. Carson stood at the fireplace.

"I can recreate these and we can turn things in our favor. We'll *own* this town." She pointed toward the coffee table, her wide sleeves fluttering around her wrists.

My eyes slid to where she pointed and my breath caught in my throat. The book Carson had taken from me lay on the table, the binding open to the middle, revealing the ink covered parchment pages.

"I don't know, Felicity. Your spells have mostly backfired, so far." Idris Bates looked at his daughter-in-law disapprovingly.

Carson coughed over by the fireplace, and the two other Bates' looked at him. "We need to make use of what's in the book if we plan to turn Mystic Notch to our side."

My eyes slid from Carson to the book. I had no idea what he meant by 'turn Mystic Notch to our side', but I had a pretty good idea it wasn't anything I would like. It all hinged on the book and I was the one that had screwed up and let Carson get ahold of it. If anything bad happened in Mystic Notch because of it, it would be my fault.

I had to make things right.

I was contemplating just how to do that when a hand clamped over my mouth and pulled me back down the passage, stifling the scream that tried to burst from my throat.

***

"Shhh ... I'm on your side."

Really? It doesn't feel like it, I thought as I clawed at whomever it was, my eyes darting wildly as he pulled me into a little alcove.

"I'll help you get the book."

That got my attention. I stopped struggling and tried to turn to see who it was.

"Promise you won't scream if I let go," he said. "If you do, the rest of them will come running and it won't be a good ending for you."

I nodded.

He let go, and I whirled around to see Derek Bates standing there with a hopeful look on his face.

"You!" I hissed.

He crossed his arms over his chest.

"I should be taking that tone with *you*," he whispered. "You accused me of killing Lavinia."

"Well, considering what I'm finding out about your family, I'm wondering if you had a hand in it," I whispered back.

The cat weaved around Derek's legs mewing softly. So, it *was* his cat. He must have been telling the truth about his reason for being in town the morning of Lavinia's death.

He saw me looking down. "Yes, this is the cat I was taking to the vets. Do you believe me?"

I nodded. "But your family ..."

Derek brushed his hand through his hair. "I didn't want to believe one of them could be the killer, even though I had my doubts. But now, with that book and all ... well, you can see why I rushed you out of the house the other day."

"Sort of," I said, still not sure what the Bates family was up to. Where they witches? And whose side was Derek on?

"I saw Carson sneak in with the book. I knew he had you downstairs. I was actually on my way down to let you out," Derek frowned at me. "How *did* you get out, anyway?"

"Would you believe magic? But not the black kind. I picked the lock and your cat led me to this passage. So you're not in on any of this with your family?" I still wasn't sure I believed him, but I had to ask.

"No." His face turned hard. "I've always been different. The black sheep of the family, so to speak. I tried to ignore their darker side—I suppose I love them in some way, but this thing with the book. I just can't let them unleash evil on Mystic Notch."

Unleash evil? That sounded bad. I was pretty sure I didn't want that to happen either.

"Okay, what do you suggest we do?" Just a few hours ago, I thought Derek was the killer and now I was considering joining forces with him. I didn't see that I had too many other choices.

"We need to get the book away from them. They think you are still locked up downstairs, so we have the element of surprise on our side."

"And just how do you propose we utilize that?"

"I have an idea." Derek glanced down the passage toward the library where we could still hear the soft hum of conversation. "Here's what we'll do."

***

My nerves tingled with anticipation as I stood at the secret door, looking into the library through one of the gaps in the boards. It looked like I was seeing the room through a tunnel and I realized that my view was between two books—the door must have been cleverly built into one of the bookcases.

I shifted my position to relieve the pressure on my leg as well as to be able to get a better view of the book on the coffee table. Reminding myself to breathe, I placed my hand—the one that wasn't burned—on the panel that would slide the door open while I waited for Derek to create the distraction that would allow me to slip into the room and steal the book.

Carson, Idris and Felicity were still discussing their dastardly plan of action, but I wasn't listening. I was too intent on waiting for the perfect moment.

"Fire!" I heard Derek yell and saw him rush into the library, standing in the doorway and pointing excitedly into the hall. "The kitchen's on fire! Everyone out!"

Carson ran out into the hall. Felicity sprang up from the couch and headed toward the door. Idris followed at a more dignified pace.

I pushed the panel, the door slid silently open and I stepped into the room, my eye trained on the book.

Idris had almost cleared the door when I was already halfway into the room. He must have remembered the book on the coffee table and he turned back toward it, his eyes growing wide when he saw me.

I ran for the book, noticing absently that a paperweight very similar to the one Elspeth had given me sat on the table beside it. Like my paperweight, this one glowed strangely, as if lit from inside.

Idris charged back into the room with surprising speed for a man his age.

A jolt of adrenalin surged through me—I knew I had to stop him. I grabbed the book and the paperweight, yelping as the paperweight seared my already burned fingers.

I aimed at Idris. Swinging the orb with all my might, I let go, watching in awe as electricity arced from my fingertips, circling the paperweight that exploded into a million pieces.

Kaboom!

My eyesight blurred. I felt the sensation of flying, then the weightlessness of falling. Hot air rushed past my face, then a bone jarring thud sent pain shooting through my body before everything went black.

Chapter Thirty-Two

A crushing weight on my chest made it hard to breathe and what little air I could get was tinged with smoke and the smell of charred wood. I opened my eyes, but it was dark. The debris I was pinned beneath made it impossible to move.

"Mew."

I tried to call out, but my voice was muffled by the debris.

"Mew ... mew ... mew ..." There was more than one cat out there. I found myself hoping they were good diggers as I tried in vain to push myself out of the pile of wood and stone I was buried in.

"Over here!"

Was that Striker?

I felt the pile shift and heard the noise of wood and stone being thrown aside. A shaft of daylight appeared and I turned my face to it, sucking in a lungful of clean air.

"Chance! Are you okay?" Striker's concerned face came into view and I nodded.

A large black cat poked his face near mine as Striker continued to dig me out. A Siamese traced its rough tongue on my nose. An orange tomcat sat off to the side, sizing me up. Weren't these

Elspeth's cats? How in the world had they gotten all the way down here?

"Willa!" Bing Thorndike came into view, his eyes ringed with compassion. "Thank God you're okay."

"Is anything broken?" Striker asked.

I tried out all my limbs, wiggling my fingers and toes. Everything seemed to work. In fact, I was surprised my leg wasn't hurting more than it was. "I don't think so."

"Okay, hold on." Striker grabbed under my arms and pulled me the rest of the way out.

"I'll take the book and keep it safe for you,' Bing said.

"Book?" I frowned in the direction Bing was looking and noticed I had an old book clutched to my chest. It looked familiar, but I couldn't quite place it. I knew it was important. Looking up at Bing's smiling face, I got the overwhelming feeling that giving him the book was the right thing to do.

I handed it over.

Bing took the book, holding it carefully, then gave me a knowing look and I felt like everything was all right even though I had no idea why.

"What happened?" Striker asked.

"I don't remember." My brows mashed together as I looked at the gaping hole in the side of the Bates mansion. There had been an explosion, obviously, but I didn't remember what I had been doing here in the first place.

"Let's get you checked out." Striker grabbed my hand and it exploded in pain.

"Ouch!" I pulled my hand back turning it over to reveal blisters and raw skin.

Striker's eyes clouded with concern, he reached for my hand again.

"Let me see." He looked it over gently. "Looks like you got a bad burn. I'm going to take you over to the ambulance and get this bandaged."

Putting his arm around me, Striker led me to the front of the house, which was loaded with police cars and an ambulance. I glanced back over my shoulder to where I'd been buried in the pile. It was out of sight of the main activity.

"How did you find me over there?" I wondered.

"The cats. I noticed a group of them and they were sniffing around the pile. That's why I investigated. Then once I got close, I smelled the peppermint and knew it was you."

My cheeks burned. Did the *Iced Fire* smell that strongly? I searched for the cats, but there were none in sight.

"Willa!" Augusta came running, her arms outstretched, enveloping me in a hug. After a few seconds she held me at arm's length, inspecting me. "Are you okay?"

"Yes. I'm fine." I looked over her shoulder where the Bates family was gathered near the front of the house, my stomach clenching as I remembered how I'd falsely accused Derek. "You're not mad at me because of this morning—"

Then I remembered seeing the scratches on Carson's arm and the ring. I grabbed Augusta's arm. "Carson is the killer!"

"I know, that's why we came." Augusta looked back at the Bates family and I could see an officer approaching them. "After you accused Derek it gave me some ideas. I took a look at the clues and realized you had the right family, but wrong brother."

"He was at the shop this morning." I wrinkled my forehead in concentration. "I don't remember much ... but he had the claw marks on his arm so he must have been the one that broke into my house!"

"I know." Augusta pulled the handcuffs from the back of her uniform. "Don't worry, we have enough evidence on him to get him for the break-in and Lavinia's murder."

Augusta turned and walked away just as Striker put something that stung on my hand.

"Ouch." I pulled away.

"This will help the burn." He pulled my hand back toward him, gently swabbing it with ointment, despite my protests.

"What were you doing up here, anyway?" he asked.

"That's a good question." I chewed my bottom lip. Why *had* I been here? "All I remember is that Carson came to the shop this morning. I saw the scratches on his arm and he was wearing a navy blue coat. But the rest is fuzzy. I might have been bringing them that book."

Striker's eyes clouded with concern.

"You don't remember? Did you hit your head?" He started feeling around my head. "Does this hurt?"

"No."

"I don't feel any bumps, but it's strange you don't remember. Maybe the trauma of the explosion." He looked at the house and then back to me. "What was that book, anyway?"

"I thought it was some old family book. I found it in a box with an old Bates' family photo album."

"So then, why did Bing take it?"

"Good question," I looked around for Bing, but he was gone. "I guess I was mistaken about it being from the Bates collection."

Over near the house, I could see Augusta putting the cuffs on Carson. He looked angry. Felicity was crying. Derek stood off to the side. Idris leaned on his cane, the picture of frailty ... except something niggled at me that he was anything but frail.

Striker turned me toward him. "You don't have to worry about them. Carson's going to jail. He's been unstable for a long time."

I thought about that. It was true he was a little strange when we were younger, but since I'd been in Massachusetts until recently, I didn't really know what he'd been up to all these years.

I watched Striker wrap a large gauze bandage on my hand. His gentle motions made my heart flutter. He secured the bandage, then put his hands on my shoulders.

"I hope you've learned not to get involved in any more investigations, or at the very least to not go off on your own." He looked over my shoulder at the gaping hole in the side of the Bates mansion. "As you can see, it can be very dangerous."

His gray eyes locked back on mine and I felt a flood of warmth at the genuine concern in them.

I nodded.

"Good. Well, I'm just glad you're okay," he said, leaning in toward me and kissing me on the lips.

My pulse skittered and my stomach flip-flopped, but this time I didn't throw up on his shoes.

Chapter Thirty-Three

I stood on the sidewalk in front of the bookstore. Pandora, who I'd picked up from the animal hospital on my way to work, lay in my arms. She must have missed me, because she was letting me hold her while she purred contentedly.

Doc Evans had assured me she would be fine with no permanent ill effects other than the kink in her tail, which she slapped against my arm lazily.

I looked up at the bright sun and closed my eyes. The storm system that had brought all the rain had moved out of the mountains and the next few days promised to be the sunny and warm New Hampshire spring days that I loved. Even the birds were encouraged, as was evidenced by their lively twittering in the bud-laden trees.

Since it was so nice, I was having the morning tête-a-tête with Bing, Josiah, Cordelia and Hattie outside instead of on the purple couches in my shop.

"Thank goodness you weren't hurt, Willa," Cordelia said as she reached over to stroke Pandora's head.

"Yes, that was a freak accident," Josiah added. "I mean, the gas explosion. Blew the front side of the Bates mansion clear off."

"Gas explosion?" I wrinkled my forehead at Josiah.

"Yeah, that's what blew the side off the Bates mansion. Well, you should know, you were there." Josiah studied me, rubbing his chin. "Why *were* you there, Willa?"

"Good question," I said.

Bing gave me a knowing look and I felt like we shared a secret about that morning. Too bad I didn't remember what it was.

"I don't know how you got caught in the rubble." Hattie sipped her coffee. "But it's a good thing you weren't actually inside the house—you could have been killed."

I smiled and nodded. Inside the house? Why did I feel like I might have been in there? I shook my head—my memory of the day was still fuzzy and the truth was I had no idea where I was when the explosion happened.

"It's such a shame about Carson," Hattie said. "Felicity is crushed."

"She's kind of an odd one, don't you think, sister?" Cordelia asked Hattie.

"They're all odd, if you ask me," Josiah said. "But at least Willa was on the right track."

"Yeah, but I still don't get it. *Why* did Carson kill Lavinia?" Cordelia asked.

"Well, you know that boy's always been a little funny." Josiah tapped the side of his head. "From what I understand, Felicity sold some family books and he got it in his head they were in the library."

"Yeah, but why not just ask Lavinia? He didn't have to *kill* her," Hattie took a sip of coffee.

"Like I said, the boy ain't right," Josiah answered. "Rumor is that he claims he's innocent, even though the police have ample evidence. They say he was in the library looking for those old family books and Lavinia surprised him and he killed her. I hear he denies it, though."

"So, if Lavinia hadn't been in town early that day, she'd still be alive," Hattie mused.

My stomach crunched and I snuggled Pandora closer despite her protesting meow ... Lavinia had been killed because of her dedication to the feral cats.

"And he broke into Willa's house for the same reason," Josiah added.

"That's right. Maggie had picked up a box of books for me, and inside I found a photo album of the Bates family. When I brought it up to the Bates' house, Carson wanted to know if there were any other books in the box with it.

"I'd told him I'd left the box at home, but made a pit-stop that afternoon to bring the box to the store. Carson wouldn't have known that, though. He would have thought they were still at my house."

"Well, it's an interesting mystery, but I'm glad it's solved." Josiah looked at his watch. "And now, I must mosey off to the barber."

He nodded at us and turned to leave.

"We'll walk with you," Cordelia said. "Hattie needs to stop in the fudge shoppe."

"Not just me." Hattie swatted at Cordelia's arm. "You ate all the penuche last time."

I smiled as the three of them walked off, leaving me standing on the sidewalk with Bing.

Bing cocked a bushy eyebrow at me. "So, you don't remember much about what happened at the Bates mansion?"

I shook my head. "Not really, but there is one thing I remember. That old book ... were you looking for it too?"

"I looked all over town for it." Bing shifted uncomfortabley then leaned closer to me. "We have to make sure it doesn't get into the wrong hands."

"You looked all over town?" I narrowed my eyes remembering how I'd passed him on the road on my way to Barry's. "So that *was* you at Barry's house the other day!"

"Yes," Bing said, then held up his hands at my look of alarm. "I wasn't the one that hurt him, though. I was there in time to save him. It was Carson that knocked him out. He was there looking for the book."

I remembered how Barry had said the books were out of order in the box. And Carson lived further out than Barry so I wouldn't have passed him on the road.

"What's so important about this book, and why do you want to keep it from Carson?" I asked Bing. "I thought the Bates' had it to begin with and Felicity sold it off by mistake."

Bing pressed his lips together. "Apparently, Felicity didn't realize the value of what she'd sold. She always was kind of ditzy and old Idris doesn't keep her well-informed. Anyway, as you know, the book wasn't at Barry's. He should suffer no ill effects from his fall."

"That's right. The book was in the box Maggie had left on my porch. The one with the Bates' family scrapbook."

"We searched all local book acquisitions and even your home earlier, but that must have been before Maggie dropped the box off."

My brows rose. "You searched my house?"

Bing looked at me apologetically. "Now, don't get all upset, we were just trying to nip things in the bud before everything blew up … no pun intended. You never even knew we were there, and of course we would never do anything to hurt you."

"But when did you do that?" The memory of the night of deep sleep after eating Elspeth's pie surfaced. Was Elspeth in on this? She certainly did have some unique qualities, like conjuring up butterflies, and she did seem to have an odd way of understanding animals. "I don't understand ... who is this *we* you keep talking about and what is this really all about?"

Bing took a deep breath. "You'll understand all that in time, Willa. For now, you know what you need to and Mystic Notch will go on as it has."

A warm smile bloomed on Bing's face as he surveyed Main Street, but I hardly had time to notice. A swirly mist had started to form outside the shop door and that could only mean one thing.

"Now, if you don't mind, I must be going," Bing said, pulling my attention from the mist long enough to see him start across the street. "See you tomorrow, Willa."

"See ya." I wasn't satisfied with his lame explanation, but didn't have time to go after him. I turned my full attention on the mist discovering, much to my surprise, there were two figures.

As the ghosts started to solidify, my attention was pulled away, yet again, by the trio of women walking down the sidewalk toward me. Pepper and Elspeth walked toward me side by side with, much to my dismay, Ophelia Withington following behind them.

"Pandora, it's so good to see you all fixed up!" Elspeth kissed Pandora on the head and tweaked her tail. Pepper rubbed her neck.

Pandora, her eye on the mist swirls that only she and I could see, wriggled in my arms to get down. I gently placed her on the ground.

"And it's good to see you all fixed up, too." Elspeth gestured toward my bandaged hand.

"Yes, I was pretty lucky," I said, glancing toward the misty swirls.

Pepper hugged me. "I'm so glad nothing bad happened to you."

"Thanks," I said to Pepper, then slid narrowed eyes over to Opheila. What was *she* doing here? I hoped she wasn't going to cause some kind of trouble about me having Pandora in the bookstore.

"Mew." Pandora, on the other hand, didn't seem to have any worries as she batted and swirled at the misty figures. My brows pulled together ... was that Robert Frost and Franklin Pierce?

It was! Which was odd, because the two of them never left the bookstore as far as I knew.

"Willa?"

I turned back to Elspeth and Pepper. "What?"

"I was just saying that Striker did a great job with your hand," Pepper gave me a knowing look and I felt my cheeks burn.

"Yes, he did." I glanced nervously at Ophelia who alternated between casting strange glances at Pandora and fiddling with something under the lapels of her wide red cape that flapped in the wind.

"That's my cat, Pandora," I said glancing back to see Franklin Pierce poke playfully at the gray cat. "She's not feral."

"Oh, dear, Willa. I'm afraid you might have heard the worst about me." Ophelia pressed her lips together. "I must apologize for acting so badly, but you see, I just wasn't myself."

"Yes, it seems Ophelia has come to a new understanding." Elspeth stepped aside as she said it and I noticed that whatever Ophelia had been doing under her cape involved something furry.

A head popped out of the top of her cape and I gasped, recognizing it as the black and white kitten with the tattered ear.

"You adopted a cat?" I stared at Ophelia incredulously.

"Yes!" Ophelia beamed, as she cooed to the little kitten snuggled inside her cape.

"It seems Ophelia had a change of mind about the feral cats," Elspeth said. "She even donated some money to help fund the shelter."

"I wonder what changed her mind," Pepper cut in, raising a brow at me and purposely taking a sip of tea from the china cup she'd brought with her.

My eyes slid from Pepper to Ophelia and back again. Had Pepper's tea concoction really changed Ophelia from nasty to nice? Maybe there was something to Pepper's herbal obsession, after all.

"Not only that, but did you hear? The library is donating the sale of one of the bronzes to help build a new shelter for the feral cats." Elspeth said. "Lavinia would have liked that."

I remembered Lavinia telling me that Ophelia had scoured the library already. I'd thought she'd been looking for the bronzes, but I guess it had something to do with cats. Or maybe she thought Lavinia was hiding information about the cats there ... either way, it didn't seem like it mattered much now.

Out of the corner of my eye, I saw another swirly mist starting to form over by the door. It was Lavinia ... and she had luggage. I watched as she pecked Robert, then Franklin, on the cheek. Then she turned to me, mouthed the words 'thank you', bent down to pet Pandora and promptly disappeared.

Robert and Franklin looked sad for a few seconds, then Franklin put his arm out, gesturing for Robert to precede him, and the two of them disappeared back into the bookstore, leaving Pandora frowning at the closed door.

"Well, we're off to get cat supplies." Elspeth started down the sidewalk.

"I do hope we can be friends now." Ophelia stuck her hand out and I shook it.

"Sure," I shrugged at Pepper who favored me with a cat-that-ate-the-canary smile.

A sheriff's car pulled to the curb with Striker at the wheel.

"Hi, Eddie," Pepper waved at him, then turned to me. "Gotta get back to my shop. See you later."

She wiggled her eyebrows at me before turning and heading off in the direction of her shop. I walked toward the car, Pandora at my heels.

"Hey, Chance." Striker smiled the smile that made his dimple show up and my heart fluttered.

"Hi." I smiled back remembering our kiss.

Pandora meowed and Striker leaned his head out to look down at her. "Hello, to you, too."

We stood there awkwardly for a few seconds. We hadn't really had a chance to talk since that kiss and I felt unusually tongue-tied. My thoughts turned to his shoes. I never did apologize for throwing up on them.

"Listen, I wanted to say how sorry I was for ruining your shoes the other day when I ... you know."

Striker laughed. "Oh, don't worry. Something tells me you'll have plenty of chances to make up for it."

And with that he winked and drove off before I could say another word.

"Meow." Pandora rubbed her face against my ankle and looked up at me, her intelligent eyes taking on more of a green tint in the bright sunlight.

I stared down at her. It almost seemed as if she was trying to tell me something, and I wondered, not for the first time, if my cat knew more about what was going on, than I did.

The End.

***

Signup for Leighann Dobbs' newsletter and be the first to know about new releases - early birds get them for the lowest possible price!

http://www.leighanndobbs.com/newsletter

A Note From The Author

Thanks so much for reading my cozy mystery "*Ghostly Paws*". I hope you liked reading it as much as I loved writing it. If you did, and feel inclined to leave a review, I really would appreciate it.

This is book one of the Mystic Notch series. I plan to write many more books with Willa, Pandora and the rest of Mystic Notch. I have several other series that I write, too - you can find out more about them on my website http://www.leighanndobbs.com.

Also, if you like cozy mysteries with ghosts, magic and cats, then you'll like my book "*Dead Wrong*" which is book one in the Blackmoore Sisters series. Set in the fictional seaside town of Noquitt Maine, the Blackmoore sisters will take you on a journey of secrets, romance and maybe even a little magic. I have an excerpt from it at the end of this book.

This book has been through many edits with several people and even some software programs, but since nothing is infallible (even the software programs) you might catch a spelling error or mistake and, if you do, I sure would appreciate it if you let me know - you can contact me at lee@leighanndobbs.com.

Oh, and I love to connect with my readers so please do visit me on facebook at http://www.facebook.com/leighanndobbsbooks

Signup to get my newest releases at a discount and notification of contests:

http://www.leighanndobbs.com/newsletter

About The Author

Leighann Dobbs discovered her passion for writing after a twenty year career as a software engineer. She lives in New Hampshire with her husband Bruce, their trusty Chihuahua mix Mojo and beautiful rescue cat, Kitty. When she's not reading, gardening or selling antiques, she likes to write romance and cozy mystery novels and novelettes which are perfect for the busy person on the go.

Find out about her latest books and how to get discounts on them by signing up at:

http://www.leighanndobbs.com/newsletter

Connect with Leighann on Facebook:
http://facebook.com/leighanndobbsbooks

More Books By Leighann Dobbs:
Blackmoore Sisters
Cozy Mystery Series
* * *

Dead Wrong
Dead & Buried
Dead Tide
Buried Secrets

Lexy Baker
Cozy Mystery Series
* * *

Lexy Baker Cozy Mystery Series Boxed Set Vol 1
(Books 1-4)

Or buy the books separately:

Killer Cupcakes
Dying For Danish
Murder, Money and Marzipan
3 Bodies and a Biscotti
Brownies, Bodies & Bad Guys
Bake, Battle & Roll
Wedded Blintz
Scones, Skulls & Scams

Kate Diamond
Adventure/Suspense Series
* * *

Hidden Agemda

***

Excerpt From Dead Wrong:

Morgan Blackmoore tapped her finger lightly on the counter, her mind barely registering the low buzz of voices behind her in the crowded coffee shop as she mentally prioritized the tasks that awaited her back at her own store.

"Here you go, one yerba mate tea and a vanilla latte." Felicity rang up the purchase, as Morgan dug in the front pocket of her faded denim jeans for some cash which she traded for the two paper cups.

Inhaling the spicy aroma of the tea, she turned to leave, her long, silky black hair swinging behind her. Elbowing her way through the crowd, she headed toward the door. At this time of morning, the coffee shop was filled with locals and Morgan knew almost all of them well enough to exchange a quick greeting or nod.

Suddenly a short, stout figure appeared, blocking her path. Morgan let out a sharp breath, recognizing the figure as Prudence Littlefield.

Prudence had a long running feud with the Blackmoore's which dated back to some sort of run-in she'd had with Morgan's grandmother when they were young girls. As a result, Prudence loved to harass and berate the Blackmoore girls in public. Morgan's eyes darted around the room, looking for an escape route.

"Just who do you think you are?" Prudence demanded, her hands fisted on her hips, legs spaced shoulder width apart. Morgan noticed she was wearing her usual knee high rubber boots and an orange sunflower scarf.

Morgan's brow furrowed over her ice blue eyes as she stared at the older woman's prune like face.

"Excuse me?"

"Don't you play dumb with me Morgan Blackmoore. What kind of concoction did you give my Ed? He's been acting plumb crazy."

Morgan thought back over the previous week's customers. Ed Littlefield *had* come into her herbal remedies shop, but she'd be damned if she'd announce to the whole town what he was after.

She narrowed her eyes at Prudence. "That's between me and Ed."

Prudence's cheeks turned crimson. Her nostrils flared. "You know what *I* think," she said narrowing her eyes and leaning in toward Morgan, "I think you're a witch, just like your great-great-great-grandmother!"

Morgan felt an angry heat course through her veins. There was nothing she hated more than being called a witch. She was a Doctor of Pharmacology with a Master Herbalist's license, not some sort of spell-casting conjurer.

The coffee shop had grown silent. Morgan could feel the crowd staring at her. She leaned forward, looking wrinkled old Prudence Littlefield straight in the eye.

"Well now, I think we know that's not true," she said, her voice barely above a whisper, "Because if I was a witch, I'd have turned you into a newt long ago."

Then she pushed her way past the old crone and fled out the coffee shop door.

Fiona Blackmoore stared at the amethyst crystal in front of her wondering how to work it into a pendant. On most days, she could easily figure out exactly how to cut and position the stone, but right now her brain was in a pre-caffeine fog.

Where was Morgan with her latte?

She sighed, looking at her watch. It was ten past eight, Morgan should be here by now, she thought impatiently.

Fiona looked around the small shop, *Sticks and Stones*, she shared with her sister. An old cottage that had been in the family for generations, it sat at one of the highest points in their town of Noquitt, Maine.

Turning in her chair, she looked out the back window. In between the tree trunks that made up a small patch of woods, she had a bird's eye view of the sparkling, sapphire blue Atlantic Ocean in the distance.

The cottage sat about 500 feet inland at the top of a high cliff that plunged into the Atlantic. If the woods were cleared, like the developers wanted, the view would be even better. But Fiona would have none of that, no matter how much the developers offered them, or how much they needed the money. She and her sisters would never sell the cottage.

She turned away from the window and surveyed the inside of the shop. One side was setup as an apothecary of sorts. Antique slotted shelves loaded with various herbs lined the walls. Dried weeds hung from the rafters and several mortar and pestles stood on the counter, ready for whatever herbal concoctions her sister was hired to make.

On her side sat a variety of gemologist tools and a large assortment of crystals. Three antique oak and glass jewelry cases displayed her creations. Fiona smiled as she looked at them. Since childhood she had been fascinated with rocks and gems so it was no surprise to anyone when she grew up to become a gemologist and jewelry designer, creating jewelry not only for its beauty, but also for its healing properties.

The two sisters vocations suited each other perfectly and they often worked together providing customers with crystal and herbal healing for whatever ailed them.

The jangling of the bell over the door brought her attention to the front of the shop. She breathed a sigh of relief when Morgan burst through the door, her cheeks flushed, holding two steaming paper cups.

"What's the matter?" Fiona held her hand out, accepting the drink gratefully. Peeling back the plastic tab, she inhaled the sweet vanilla scent of the latte.

"I just had a run in with Prudence Littlefield!" Morgan's eyes flashed with anger.

"Oh? I saw her walking down Shore road this morning wearing that god-awful orange sunflower scarf. What was the run-in about this time?" Fiona took the first sip of her latte, closing her eyes and waiting for the caffeine to power her blood stream. She'd had her own run-ins with Pru Littlefield and had learned to take them in stride.

"She was upset about an herbal mix I made for Ed. She called me a witch!"

"What did you make for him?"

"Just some Ginkgo, Ginseng and Horny Goat Weed … although the latter he said was for Prudence."

Fiona's eyes grew wide. "Aren't those herbs for impotence?"

Morgan shrugged "Well, that's what he wanted."

"No wonder Prudence was mad...although you'd think just being married to her would have caused the impotence."

Morgan burst out laughing. "No kidding. I had to question his sanity when he asked me for it. I thought maybe he had a girlfriend on the side."

Fiona shook her head trying to clear the unwanted images of Ed and Prudence Littlefield together.

"Well, I wouldn't let it ruin my day. You know how *she* is."

Morgan put her tea on the counter, then turned to her apothecary shelf and picked several herbs out of the slots. "I know, but she always seems to know how to push my buttons. Especially when she calls me a witch."

Fiona grimaced. "Right, well I wish we *were* witches. Then we could just conjure up some money and not be scrambling to pay the taxes on this shop and the house."

Morgan sat in a tall chair behind the counter and proceeded to measure dried herbs into a mortar.

"I know. I saw Eli Stark in town yesterday and he was pestering me about selling the shop again."

"What did you tell him?"

"I told him we'd sell over our dead bodies." Morgan picked up a pestle and started grinding away at the herbs.

Fiona smiled. Eli Stark had been after them for almost a year to sell the small piece of land their shop sat on. He had visions of buying it, along with some adjacent lots in order to develop the area into high end condos.

Even though their parents early deaths had left Fiona, Morgan and their two other sisters property rich but cash poor the four of them agreed they would never sell. Both the small shop and the stately ocean home they lived in had been in the family for generations and they didn't want *their* generation to be the one that lost them.

The only problem was, although they owned the properties outright, the taxes were astronomical and, on their meager earnings, they were all just scraping by to make ends meet.

All the more reason to get this necklace finished so I can get paid. Thankfully, the caffeine had finally cleared the cobwebs in her head and Fiona was ready to get to work. Staring down at the amethyst, a vision of the perfect shape to cut the stone appeared in her mind. She grabbed her tools and started shaping the stone.

Fiona and Morgan were both lost in their work. They worked silently, the only sounds in the little shop being the scrape of mortar on pestle and the hum of Fiona's gem grinding tool mixed with a few melodic tweets and chirps that floated in from the open window.

Fiona didn't know how long they were working like that when the bell over the shop door chimed again. She figured it must have been an hour or two judging by the fact that the few sips left in the bottom of her latte cup had grown cold.

She smiled, looking up from her work to greet their potential customer, but the smile froze on her face when she saw who it was.

Sheriff Overton stood in the door flanked by two police officers. A toothpick jutted out of the side of Overton's mouth and judging by the looks on all three of their faces, they weren't there to buy herbs or crystals.

Fiona could almost hear her heart beating in the silence as the men stood there, adjusting their eyes to the light and getting their bearings.

"Can we help you?" Morgan asked, stopping her work to wipe her hands on a towel.

Overton's head swiveled in her direction like a hawk spying a rabbit in a field.

"That's her." He nodded to the two uniformed men who approached Morgan hesitantly. Fiona recognized one of the men as Brody Hunter, whose older brother Morgan had dated all through high school. She saw Brody look questioningly at the Sheriff.

The other man stood a head taller than Brody. Fiona noticed his dark hair and broad shoulders but her assessment of him stopped there when she saw him pulling out a pair of handcuffs.

Her heart lurched at the look of panic on her sister's face as the men advanced toward her.

"Just what is this all about?" She demanded, standing up and taking a step toward the Sheriff.

There was no love lost between the Sheriff and Fiona. They'd had a few run-ins and she thought he was an egotistical bore and probably crooked too. He ignored her question focusing his attention on Morgan. The next words out of his mouth chilled Fiona to the core.

"Morgan Blackmoore ... you're under arrest for the murder of Prudence Littlefield."

35428925R00170

Made in the USA
Middletown, DE
03 October 2016